Elemental Superpowers

THE MUDPIE

A.J. LLEWELLYN and SERENA YATES

The Mudpie
ISBN # 978-1-78184-550-9
©Copyright A.J. Llewellyn and Serena Yates 2012
Cover Art by Posh Gosh ©Copyright September 2012
Interior text design by Claire Siemaszkiewicz
Total-E-Bound Publishing

Praise for

A.J. Llewellyn and Serena Yates

'The Mudpie' is an amusing, tongue-in-cheek, but sometimes quite serious fantasy love story...Thanks, A.J. and Serena, for another wonderful supernatural adventure. ~ *Rainbow Book Reviews*

Total-E-Bound Publishing books by A.J. Llewellyn and Serena Yates:

The Cake
The Blancmange
The Mudpie

THE MUDPIE

Dedication

To all those who agree that life — like mudpie — is a multi-layered thing.

"Boys, set the terror level at code brown, 'cause I need to change my pants."

— the President of the United States, Monsters vs. Aliens.

Chapter One

"Okay, Mitchell. Blow through this crystal."

Mitchell Dykins hesitated. So far, so weird. Well, the office wasn't weird, now that he was used to breathing through the haze of *nag champa* incense. The half-grimy windows held a wonderful view of San Francisco's Golden Gate Bridge beneath the sun, which shone in a pale egg-yellow outside. The office itself was artfully cluttered with all kinds of Native American ephemera and piles of books. A couple of cats lay sleeping on stacks of old newspapers.

It could have been a cosy setting except that he hadn't been offered a cup of tea or a cookie. He tried to relax. He felt a bit stupid, and yet oddly excited at the same time. He had never thought about soul retrieval, never even *heard* of it until his sister Alicia insisted he try it. She'd even sprung for the hefty two hundred dollar fee. She knew he really couldn't afford it since he'd been unemployed for months. Now that he was firmly back in the grip of the workforce, he was busy paying off credit-card debt. His only luxuries were some essential clothing items for his astonishing new job.

Yes, he was employed, but, as Alicia loved to point out, his crippling self-doubts could easily cause him to self-sabotage at a moment's notice. As shocked as he was by his new, lucrative position as head of marketing for World Wide Wrestlers, Inc., he panicked every waking moment that he'd somehow manage to screw it up.

He reached across the desk, hiding his doubts and taking the small, thinly sliced yellow geode crystal from the therapist's fingers. The outside edge was a rough, greyish stone, the crystal itself a dazzling yellow disappearing into a hollow centre.

Carrie Hoffman was a soul retriever. He knew only three people in the whole of the US did this work and she was one of them. He didn't fully understand what it meant, but he was willing to go along with things…for now.

They'd talked twice by phone and exchanged emails. She'd asked six pertinent questions about why he needed soul retrieval.

He'd tamped down his inclination to type back—*I don't. My sister thinks I need it.* Instead, he'd written the truth—*I've overcome severe depression and my life seems on an upswing but I am afraid I'll sink back into the abyss. I've been this way my whole life and I don't know why.*

Mitchell felt an odd tug of emotion he couldn't identify. Carrie had asked him to delay a business trip to New York to be in her office for the session. She often worked remotely but she'd requested his presence for this particular soul retrieval. She said she'd meditated on it and that her 'guides' said he needed to be with her.

He had been nervous but had granted her three requests — to be in her office by ten a.m., to clear his schedule for the day and not to deal with any business for that duration, and to go straight home and rest afterwards. She had strongly advised him not to have dinner with business associates or friends with problems.

"You'll want to walk with nature afterwards. Hug a tree. Be as quiet as possible."

She was a matronly, mothering type of woman, with long, flowing honey-coloured hair. Their colouring was so similar she could have been his mother. She, however, was very feminine and wore interesting jewellery. She also had a nice smell he couldn't identify. She was earthy and sweet. Instinctively, he trusted her.

He was about to pucker up and blow into the crystal when she spoke again.

"Mitchell, I want you to know, I am on this journey with you. You are not alone."

He nodded.

"We are about to return to a traumatic scene in your childhood. Whatever happened to you was so devastating that you have buried it deep in your subconscious."

"But I don't remember anything happening to me when I was a kid. I had a marvellous childhood," he blurted.

She gave him a sympathetic smile. She kind of reminded him of Dr. Drew, the man who treated celebrity drunks. He got that same expression, a mixture of pain and pity on his face.

"You've forgotten, my dear. That's why you're here." She paused, as if hunting for the right words. "What happens is that, when we are presented with a harrowing experience, we lose pieces of our soul. They break off like chunks of ice and drift out to psychic islands…as a way of protecting us from further spiritual and emotional damage."

He nodded. He had heard that people who suffered sexual abuse couldn't remember specific details…but nothing like that had ever happened to him.

"…only those pieces of our soul never come back. They don't know how. This work I am doing started when I helped another young man like yourself." She beamed at him over her granny glasses. "Now, blow."

Mitchell blew. She urged him to try it a second time. Then a strange thing happened. The cats asleep in the room sat up and both jumped from their perches. One wrapped its legs around him and he found himself propelled forwards. He had the weirdest sensation of falling…falling into darkness.

Carrie's voice came to him like an echo behind his head. He panicked for a moment when he felt as if he were trapped in a well. He blinked when he saw grass emerging under his feet. The two cats leapt ahead of him then bunnies hopped across his path as he suddenly landed on what felt like a polished, wooden floor. It wasn't a physical sensation, but a visual one. He heard himself breathing, heard the stress in his sharp exhalations.

He was standing in the back of a church. He squinted as his eyes adjusted to the darkness. He recognised the church…from where? He was not a religious man. He hadn't been inside a church since he was a kid, but the stained-glass windows on both sides seemed to stir a memory of something he'd once cherished. He started to hear voices now. He peered down the aisle and gasped.

Sister Mary Frances Rose. Man! He hadn't thought about that nasty old nun in years.

He blinked. *My God...it's my classmates all laughing and chatting in the front row...*

Mitchell felt hot tears pricking his eyes when his gaze fell on a figure at the end of the row. Mitchell couldn't breathe for a moment. He remembered now. *My God, I look like I'm frozen. I look as if I've been carved from ice.*

His head dropped. He remembered and couldn't believe this was happening to him. He'd gone to a strict Catholic school and had come to church for Holy Communion. They'd all been excited. He'd been ten years old, alive with all the possibilities life had in store for him.

Mitchell blinked again. He saw feet beside him. Shadowy figures stood with him and behind him.

He couldn't see faces. They were silhouettes in his mind until he caught a glimpse of his Uncle George who'd died when Mitchell was nine. He became so emotional when he saw his beloved uncle's face that tears streaked down his face.

At the front of the church, Sister Mary Frances Rose admonished the children for talking.

"Stop!" she yelled. "Stop now or you won't receive your Holy Communion and your soul will rot in hell...you horrible little children!"

Mitchell watched as she walked down the line, picking on him, of all people. "You! Mitchell Dykins. No Holy Communion for you! Get out of this church. *Now!*"

With the memory of a child's shame, Mitchell's legs trembled as he watched. Oh, the humiliation! His classmates had been shocked. Nobody had *ever* been forbidden from receiving Holy Communion before.

His heart broke for the little boy he'd been as the nun kept screeching at him.

"Heathen! Devil!"

Carrie Hoffman's voice spoke over the awful event.

"Mitchell, I'm going to ask one of your guides, one of your ancestors who is standing with you, to help now. They always come from behind you. Do you understand?"

He nodded, unable to speak thanks to his racking tears that threatened to choke him.

Carrie's voice sounded clear and calm. "If there is an ancestor here who loves Mitchell and wants to help him receive Holy Communion, please step forward."

Nothing.

She asked a second time.

Nothing. None of the shadowy figures moved.

Holy shit! None of my ancestors loves me enough to come forward. I'm totally screwed!

Then…a figure…a light, a bright splendid being that Mitchell could see out of the corner of his left eye moved down the left side of the church.

Mitchell stared through a veil of tears. He saw it, but he didn't believe it.

The beautiful, white bright angel pushed past all the souls of the ancestors and moved with ease and grace. He filled the church with his love. Mitchell could feel it through every cell in his body.

"Oh, my God," Carrie moaned, "it's…*him!*"

In his thirty years on Earth, Mitchell had never seen anything more beautiful.

It was Jesus of Nazareth. But Mitchell wasn't a believer. How could this be?

"I will give Mitchell his Holy Communion," the angel's deep, resonant voice announced.

Jesus of Nazareth stood in front of the child Mitchell, and Mitchell the adult watched himself unfreeze. Something weird began to happen to him. For twenty years he'd suppressed his anguish. He suddenly felt seasick. And the next thing he knew, he was back in Carrie's office, one lone tear still tumbling down his face.

"Was that real?" he asked, his voice thick.

"Yes. Oh, yes, it was real." She came around to him. "Are you okay?"

"I don't know." His head kept spinning and he felt very ill. Awful memories of that hideous day, long quashed, came flooding back.

She chewed her bottom lip a moment. "Lie down on the sofa. You look quite…green."

He let her lead him like a small, awkward kid to the sofa. It smelt like cats and mothballs but he didn't care. She gave him a tissue and a glass of water. He felt better after he blew his nose. He sipped at the water and she took the glass from his shaky hands.

"Lie down," she urged. "Close your eyes. Try not to think."

Try not to think? That was a laugh. He lay back, his head still doing its own Irish jig.

Carrie perched beside him on the sofa.

"Mitchell, I very rarely allow clients to experience the moment of psychic separation when something has impacted them so strongly."

"I can't believe it was that incident. I feel like worse things have happened to me."

She was quiet for a moment. She placed a cool cloth over his closed eyes and his head felt a little better.

"Who else was affected by Sister Mary Frances Rose's refusal to allow you to receive Communion?"

"Oh!" he gasped. "My mother."

They'd been living in New York at the time. Holy cow, even the address came back to him—ten Marley Place in east midtown.

"She was so mad," he remembered. Publicly she'd been outraged with his teacher, but in private she'd punished Mitchell. She'd even taken away his beloved puppy, Mitzi. He never knew what had become of that fluffy brown dog. Oh, God, he'd forgotten her all these years. His mother had never told him the truth, not even when she was really snockered.

Carrie kept her hand on his head. "We all experience life steps that cause us to have more little chunks of ice to fall away. I've isolated four other situations that impacted you severely. Most of them, however, were before you were eighteen. These incidents sent your soul pieces to the island of lost boys."

He gave a hoot of derision. "Island of lost boys? This sounds like a fairy tale."

"You're a very sensitive man, Mitchell. And yes, it exists. I will release your remaining soul parts without telling you what they are. I've found that my clients tend to focus on the bad experience, rather than the incredible sensation of pieces of their soul coming back. "

"Then why did you make me go through this?" he asked, unable to keep the anger from his tone.

"Because I wanted you to understand the root of the depth of your despair. Without it, you might try to take your own life again and I can't imagine a bigger waste, Mitchell. You're a really wonderful person."

Oh, my God…how does she know?

"Did my sister tell you?"

"No." She began to stroke his head. "I saw it when I started going into a trance. Please listen to me, Mitchell. You deserve to be loved. I know you've been through hell. Let me help you find a little bit of heaven now."

He didn't know what to say. He started to cry again.

"Come, Tully," Carrie said to the big black cat that had settled on his feet without Mitchell realising it. He could hear the animal's soft purring as they moved away from him. He fell into a deep sleep in the middle of his thoughts. He was aware he was dreaming and yet he seemed to hover outside of himself, watching his physical form.

He gazed outside the therapist's windows and saw something strange.

The Golden Gate Bridge was no longer in view.

What he could see now was a giant mudpit.

Then the world went black.

* * * *

"Stop."

Mitchell stopped. He and a group of about fifty others had been held up for the last half-hour at San Francisco Airport by TSA officials and forced to go slowly through the body-scanning machines. It seemed like some huge power play. Not that he minded. Unusual for him. He hated not being in control of any situation, but somehow he felt relaxed and calm, as if he'd just had a two-hour massage.

Now they'd all emerged from the scanner, anxious to make it to their boarding gates before their flights left without them. However, Mitchell and several others had been forced to remain, watching the rest of the group scurrying up the escalators.

They'd halted so suddenly, the man behind Mitchell slammed right into him.

"Oops…sorry." The guy's crotch pressed into Mitchell's ass, but soon moved away again. The intimate contact startled Mitchell. *Man, I'm so hard up I'm reading a come-on into everything.*

He turned, caught the man's disarming grin and returned it.

Then they waited. Mitchell longed to turn back and stare some more, but it would have been rude. Wouldn't it? The man was gorgeous. He exuded a strong sexual chemistry that Mitchell felt right away. A second quick glance in which Mitchell pretended to scan the others around him revealed that the hot guy had long, flowing, gleaming shoulder-length chestnut hair and brown eyes that made Mitchell think of…chocolate mudpie.

What the heck was wrong with him? Mitchell had had a strange evening alone in his Mission district apartment. He'd felt high…exhilarated, yet disconnected from himself. He'd spent the evening quietly, listening to Fitz and the Tantrums, eating cold, homemade udon noodles and strawberries, the only things he could find in his fridge. Just when he was contemplating ordering takeout, his boss, Larry Parker, had called and asked him to take the red-eye to New York.

Larry hated his name since it was the same one as a famous ambulance-chasing attorney whose ads had run for years across the US—'Hi, I'm Larry H. Parker and I'll fight for you!' Mitchell's Larry was always mistaken for *the* Larry and people pestered him with their gruesome accident stories. Mitchell had taken the day off saying he had medical issues to deal with, which was sort of true, and after a cursory enquiry into Mitchell's well-being, Larry trampled Mitchell's response, demanding he be at a nine a.m. press conference the next day at the company's New York City midtown offices.

Mitchell had created a line of old-fashioned bubblegum trading cards featuring World Wide Wrestlers, Inc.'s biggest stars. He'd selected a retro Seventies style and the fans had gone wild. Mitchell knew which of the fifty-five featured wrestlers were the most popular. He'd gone to great lengths to interview each performer. He especially loved the mud wrestlers. There were sixteen, but his favourite was Whip 'Mudshark' Jackson.

He broke from his reverie when the TSA security people allowed them up the escalator towards the gates. They didn't get far. They were stopped again, between escalators. There seemed to be no good reason for it. It was all about control. It was weird. A few days ago, Mitchell would have flipped out. He hated people arbitrarily forcing their will on him. Now, he didn't much care. He was too busy thinking about his session with Carrie.

His sleepiness had precluded him from experiencing the rest of the session but she had promised to send him the tape, plus some tools to help him process the experience. She told him she would record some meditation exercises to help him work through his fears.

"What I've done is returned your missing soul parts," she said. "But you have to work, too. You don't want them floating away again, so it's important you be very gentle with yourself."

She had told him, to his dismay, that beyond the tape she'd be sending him, he could not call or email her for advice or comfort. He already felt a little adrift. He'd had no experience with this kind of procedure before, but she said the tape would explain everything.

"I only do two sessions a week," she said. "It's a lot for me to take on. I love to help but I can't do more than I do." She had said that in the unlikely event he needed a second retrieval, he could book one in twelve months. She had given him the crystal he'd blown into, telling him the touchstone would help him feel grounded. He was beginning to think the crystal would be more of a reminder that the session had been *real*.

As he stood and waited, his fingers rubbed over the crystal's smooth surface, his fingernail worrying the jagged edges of the hole in the centre of it. He remembered the feeling of falling down a well and dropped the crystal back in his pocket.

They all charged forwards to their departure gate with seconds to spare. Mitchell and a few others handed their boarding passes to the ground crew of Virgin Atlantic for yet another inspection then stampeded down the long portable tunnel to their aircraft. He was flying business class, which surprised him. Larry had made use of his own frequent-flyer miles as a small reward for Mitchell for all his hard work.

He slid into his luxurious, spacious leather seat, pleased he had some leg room. At five feet eleven inches, he wasn't a very tall man but it would be nice not to have the person in front of him bashing his head the second he reclined his seat.

Mitchell opened the messenger bag containing all of his electronic gadgets and flipped open his tray table. He pulled out the small plastic bag containing the prototype for a new set of cards. Mitchell and his sister Alicia had created them together, complete with a PowerPoint display he would show the investors in the morning. He looked at all the Mud stars on the cards. They had proven to be the most popular wrestlers of all. The photos had yet to be approved by the participants, but they were, after all, only mock-ups.

He studied the photo of Whip 'Mudshark' Jackson and stifled some drool. The man had a magnificent body. He was hotter than hot. He had cheek-length, straggly but sexy dark hair, a permanent three-day growth and he always wrestled almost naked in nothing but teeny, tiny white underpants with a picture of a hand grenade stretched across his cock. Oh, boy, he was hot.

"What an ego," a voice beside him said.

"Excuse me?" Mitchell looked up to find the handsome guy who'd bumped into him in the terminal.

"What an ego." The guy gestured at the trading card. "I've seen Mudshark Jackson interviewed and he's a jackass."

Mitchell sort of privately agreed that Mudshark had a bit of an ego, but he also had huge fantasies about him. Besides, he wouldn't engage in trash-talking about one of his own.

"He's a confident man, not a jackass."

"No. He's a jackass." The other guy tapped his iPhone. "Never seen a bigger ego on a guy."

"He's very nice, actually." Mitchell didn't know Mudshark but had never heard anything bad about him. He knew the guy took his stuff seriously. He worked out every day and turned up on time to all his appointments for the company. Mitchell had never heard about the guy partying or dating endless coteries of models and behaving badly in public.

Their contact had been minimal, by phone and email, but Whip Jackson had always been professional, courteous and, unlike some wrestlers, returned all his proofed PR materials in a timely manner.

Mitchell started putting his cards back into the baggie. Mindful that these were prototypes, he knew they were confidential. The cards fell everywhere. God! Mitchell cursed himself, scrambling to collect them all as his cell phone rang.

"You on board the flight?" Larry hollered into his ear.

"Yes. Don't shout."

Mitchell and a few others picked up the cards. The man beside him had grabbed a couple and was scrutinising them. Mitchell held his hand out. The guy gave him a scornful glance and returned his attention to the cards. Mitchell snatched them right out of his fingers as Larry said, "Bad news on the hotel front. I wasn't really able to get you a decent hotel at short notice. But I booked you into the Hotel Carter. I'll text you the addy. It's only two nights. You'll survive."

"Thanks," Mitchell said. What had Larry meant by 'you'll survive'?

He ended the call just as the pilot announced that all passengers should turn off all electronic devices. He kept emphasising *all*. Their flight attendant stood over the guy beside him until the man turned off his iPhone. He turned it right back on again as soon as she'd left his seat.

Mitchell counted his cards. One was missing. *Hotel Carter*. Now why was that name familiar? He'd heard of it but in relation to what? He thought about this as he hunted for the missing card. *Damn*. He couldn't find it.

"Looking for this?" Mr. Unpleasant beside him asked, holding up Mitchell's quarry.

"Yes," he said, relieved. "Thanks."

The man tossed it to him. Mitchell caught it and stuck it into the bag with the others.

"So, you know Mudshark Jackson and you don't think he's an ass?"

"No, of course he's not an ass. He's a brilliant performer."

"Doesn't mean he's not an ass."

"No. He's not an ass." Why was the guy pushing this?

"Well, I think he's an ass. A pompous ass."

"No, he's not." This guy was beginning to bug Mitchell. He found himself growing more vehement. "He's always been nice to me." Mitchell felt hot under the collar and damp in his armpits. Man...you could walk out of the house with every good intention to have a nice day. All it took was one clown to muck it all up.

He was about to tell this guy who the real jackass was when his neighbour gave him a quizzical look.

"And you are?"

"Excuse me?"

"I want to know who you are."

"Who am I?"

"Yeah. As in, what is your name?" He enunciated his words carefully as if Mitchell were very stupid.

"Um..." Mitchell suddenly couldn't think. This man might be unpleasant but he made Mitchell's insides turn liquid. *Christ, I have to start jacking off more. I'm acting like a horny teenager.*

"Mitchell."

"Mitchell what?"

Why does he want to know? Knowing Mitchell was representing his company he responded with the truth. "Dykins."

The man stared at him a moment, then grinned. Mitchell found himself panting with pleasure.

"Nice to meet you, Mitchell. I'm Whip Jackson."

Mitchell thought if his mouth hung open any longer he'd maybe catch a few flies. He stared at Whip. "You don't look like yourself." *Oh, man…talk about dumbass lines of the year.*

Whip laughed. "Like you said, I'm a brilliant performer."

And a jackass…

Whip stared at Mitchell. His eyes were really beautiful. "I'm trying to figure out how I know you. I don't think we've met. I'm sure I'd remember such a huge fan."

"Well, no. I'm, um…the marketing director for World Wide."

"Oh, right. I think we've spoken a couple of times."

You only think *we've spoken? I must have made a great impression on you…* "Yes, we have."

"Well, thanks for defending my honour. What are those cards you have in your bag?"

"New prototypes for a special Mud pack."

Whip lifted a brow. "Nobody sent them to me for approval yet."

"Like I said, it's a prototype. Once the big cheese endorses it, you'll get to look at the cards and approve them."

"I like them. Mine makes my cock look nice and big. Don't you think?"

Mitchell didn't know what to say.

Whip started laughing. "You should see your face." He turned his attention to his iPad, which he'd just turned on. Mitchell watched the man tap his iBooks app and open a book. What did a professional mud wrestler read?

Mud, Sweat, and Tears – The Legend of Whip 'Mudshark' Jackson.

Oh, boy…he's reading his own memoirs!

Whip glanced at him. "Are you the one who authorised this book?"

A little embarrassed to be caught staring, Mitchell shook his head. "No. I didn't even know there was a book about you."

Whip gave him a funny look. "Glad you weren't behind this. It's the silliest book I ever read."

Mitchell burst out laughing. Whip joined him.

"Champagne?" their flight attendant asked.

They both accepted.

"Cheers," Whip said, clinking his flute against Mitchell's.

Mitchell took a couple of appreciative sips and, feeling emboldened, glanced at Whip. "What's wrong with the book?"

"Glad you asked." Whip's eyes gleamed appreciatively. "Here. You read it and tell me what you think."

He slid his iPad over to Mitchell who was about to protest, but Whip cut him off. "Don't worry. It's short. Apparently, there isn't much to my legend." He chuckled, slipping earbuds into his ears before connecting the cord to the armrest. He closed his eyes. Evidently, their conversation was over.

Mitchell read the book, cringing at some of the descriptions of Mudshark Jackson. The few minutes he'd spent with the man told Mitchell that Whip had a wicked sense of humour but this didn't come across in the book. He was a little surprised to read of the man's early beginnings on his parents' dairy farm. He'd been forced to work from the age of three, milking the cows and tending the calves. He was further amazed to learn that the young Whip Jackson used to hide the calves in his bedroom on slaughter days.

He was stunned by the older Whip's adult exploits, such as wrestling an anaconda and a crocodile, defeating them both with his trademark karate chop, but the biggest surprise was the absence of any mention of a love life.

"Well, what do you think?" Whip asked when Mitchell reached the last page. He must have been watching Mitchell, waiting for him to finish reading.

"Did you really kill an anaconda?"

"Of course not."

"But—"

"I believe they lifted all that crap straight from the autobiography of Errol Flynn. Good thing the man's dead. He could sue my ass off."

Mitchell laughed. Whip Jackson was quite a character.

"Did you really hide the calves on slaughter day?"

The man's whole face changed. He frowned. "Yes." A beat. "What else?"

Mitchell shrugged. "You are apparently all work and no play."

"Yeah. You noticed that. I don't know how to remedy it. You're the marketing guy. I mean, I don't want to pretend I'm straight. I'm no rabid skirt-chaser, but on the other hand, will the fans accept a gay Mudshark?"

Mitchell stared at him. Mudshark Jackson was gay? *Yee-ha!*

The flight attendant's announcement that they were about to land at JFK saved him from a response.

Mitchell looked around him, stunned. "We're landing? Already? What happened to food service?"

"You missed it. I got the filet mignon." Whip smacked his lips in appreciation. "Mighty tasty, too."

Chapter Two

Whip Jackson struggled to keep up with Mitchell's stride. The guy had a vibe — an open, direct quality in sharp contrast with the way he dressed. He seemed to hide his handsomeness by buttoning every last button on his shirt and constantly looking down or away the moment he made eye contact with anybody. His clothing was immaculate and decidedly conservative. The man even had a crease in his jeans, for God's sake. From what he could see, Mitchell had a nice body with a swagger to his stride. Whip found himself smiling.

Mitchell Dykins was probably a wild tiger in the sack. At first glance he was a buttoned-up guy, in more ways than one. Underneath that proper Abercrombie & Fitch shirt, there was probably another 'buttoned-up shirt'…yet something about Mitchell intrigued him. The way he'd defended Mudshark impressed Whip. It had surprised him because Whip more than suspected most of the staff at World Wide Wrestlers, Inc. hated him. Whip had a problem. He could read people's minds. He knew what they were thinking...most of the time. Surprisingly, he'd been hardly able to read Mitchell and that made him more interesting to Whip.

Nothing turned him on more than bedding a proper-looking, possibly frightened man and making him come hard.

He caught up with Mitchell, transferring his overnight bag to his left shoulder.

"So where's the ambulance chaser got you holed up?"

Mitchell, who was rifling through his cell phone's text messages, flashed him a smile. Hot *damn*! He was right. Underneath that earthy exterior beat a hot, volcanic heart. Whip was certain of it. Mitchell was fine. Whip's breath caught in his throat. Mitchell might be smiling now but Whip knew from the man's hurt-looking eyes that he had known the darkness.

"Ambulance chaser. God, how funny!" Mitchell held up his phone. "He's booked me into the Hotel Carter."

"You're shitting me." Whip couldn't believe it.

"I shit you not. I was wondering how I knew the name. I just Googled it. I think I'm afraid to go there."

Whip stifled a desire to laugh. "Yeah, you should be. It's topped the list of worst hotels in America three years in a row."

"Yeah, so I just discovered. I was reading some reviews on TripAdvisor. One lady just posted photos from her hotel room. She found bloodstains on the walls."

He handed the phone to Whip, who shook his head. "You can't stay there, Mitchell."

Mitchell shrugged.

"I'm serious." Whip just knew Mitchell wouldn't be safe there. Or comfortable. "It has all the ambience of a prison camp." He felt guilty when he added, "He's booked me into The Meridien."

Mitchell looked devastated. "That's supposed to be a nice hotel."

"Yeah. One of the best." Whip knew what to do now so he stopped and grabbed Mitchell's arm. "You're gonna have to stay with me."

"I can't—" Mitchell looked horrified.

"Why not? You got a jealous boyfriend back home, or something?"

"No boyfriend. Not even close, but..." Mitchell turned bright red.

Probably he realised he'd just outed himself. Not just as gay but dateless. *Oh, heck.* Not that it mattered — after all, Whip had outed himself too.

"Come on, guy. You missed dinner and I'm always hungry. It's wrestling all those alligators, you know." What was it going to take to convince Mitchell?

A wide grin from Mitchell indicated possible progress.

"Let's grab a bite to eat. I know a cool little place that serves great breakfast. We can go check in, freshen up and head to the meeting."

Mitchell hesitated.

"Look, nobody needs to know we're fraternising. In case you hadn't noticed, I keep my private life private." Not that he'd mind sharing certain parts with Mitchell.

"I'd noticed." Mitchell gazed at him a moment. "Okay, I'll take you up on your kind offer."

"Don't get all gooey on me," Whip said, regretting his words instantly. Mitchell's smile vanished, the pain and uncertainty returning to the man's eyes. There was something...fragile about Mitchell that worried him. It was both endearing yet disconcerting. What the hell had happened to him?

Whip tried to cover up his harsh tone with a grin. "It's just a hotel room. Minus bloodstains. One hopes."

Mitchell laughed, the smile back on his face. "If not...I can always post it to TripAdvisor. Kidding!"

It was five a.m. when they grabbed a taxi and headed towards Manhattan. Whip appreciated the fact that Mitchell was the same kind of traveller he was. Light and compact. Most gay men Whip knew had a suitcase just for their toiletries. He instructed the driver to take them to a place called Fluffy's on Seventh Avenue. He hadn't been there in a while, but with its red awnings and scent of coffee wafting out the door it hit all of his on-buttons. He could tell it hit Mitchell's too, in just the right way.

For the first time since they'd met, Whip read one of Mitchell's thoughts.

I think it's funny that such a macho guy as Whip would pick a place with a name like Fluffy's.

Hmm... Whip took slight offence.

"You've got a company expense account, right, Mitchypoo? You get the cab. Breakfast is on me."

Mitchell passed the driver his credit card as Whip exited the vehicle. Whip could tell by the tight lines around Mitchell's mouth that his travelling companion *hated* being called Mitchypoo.

"Tip him big, Mitchypoo," Whip said. "He deserves a reward for the nice-smelling cab. I'll go grab us a table."

Mitchell paid up, thanked the driver and followed Whip inside. Whip kept an eye on the guy, ordering them both coffee. He was arranging Mitchell's cup across from him with sugar and cream and realised Mitchell might find it strange that Whip knew he didn't drink decaf. All his life, Whip had found it hard to explain his own weird phenomena. He sometimes just *knew* things. He had used it to his advantage, but never illegally. He didn't refrain from relying on it to overcome his opponents in wrestling, but wrestling was just the beginning. Whip planned on being a multidimensional entertainer.

For the second time, he read Mitchell's thoughts. Apparently, it surprised Mitchell that Whip would be so thoughtful getting him coffee and cream.

Wow, I must come across as a real asshole. Aloud he said, "I hope you drink fully leaded coffee. You want pancakes, or are you an omelette guy?"

"Both."

"Me too."

They placed their orders, the café filling quickly with groups of female friends who could have been straight out of *Sex and the City*. He tuned to Mitchell again. He was surprised to find that Mitchell was thinking the same damned thing about the women in the café. Both of them could pick out the Carries, Mirandas and Charlottes among them.

Whip wanted to say something about that, but was afraid of spooking Mitchell. He picked a safer topic to hold the man's attention.

"I owe you an apology." Whip was working on his second cup of coffee as their very fluffy buttermilk and banana pancakes arrived.

"Me?"

Whip read the man's thoughts again.

I can think of a couple of reasons Whip owes me an apology. Mitchypoo being one of them.

Whip almost laughed because Mitchell kept such a benign expression on his face, fully attentive to Whip.

"When you interviewed me for the trading cards I wasn't very forthcoming with you and I do feel a bit ashamed of myself."

"You do?" Mitchell seemed to think about this for a moment. "I thought you were direct and quite…honest."

"Except for the part about why I chose the wrestling name of Mudshark."

Mitchell grinned. "That didn't really bother me. I figured it meant something to you…something deeply personal."

"You could say that. Did you ever hear the urban legend about Led Zeppelin fishing for mudsharks on Puget Sound back in the sixties when they were in Seattle for a concert festival?"

"No. Can't say that I have." Mitchell frowned, forking the strawberry garnish on his plate. "Oh…wait. I did. But I heard a wild story about how they, er…used a mudshark's snout on a groupie."

Whip grinned. "You must be a music fan."

"I am. You must be one, too." Mitchell looked almost relieved.

Whip nodded, agreeing that he was, indeed, a music fan. He finished off his pancake, using his fork to scrape the last ribbon of maple syrup from his plate, then leant back in his chair.

"Yeah…there's a ton of stories—conflicting ones—from that tour. The one that bugged me was that they caught the sharks and put them on coat hangers in their closets." He shuddered with the memory.

"Oh." Mitchell grimaced. "I didn't hear that one."

"Mudsharks are misunderstood creatures. Every time I wrestle, I feel like I'm helping those poor docile creatures fight back." He leant forwards, elbows on the table. "How come I never see you at my wrestling matches, Mitchell? How come I've never met you before?"

"Oh, I'm there. Every time. You just don't notice me." Mitchell went for the cheque but Whip grabbed it.

"Nope. This one's on me." Whip left a couple of twenties on the charge plate and stood. "Are you ready?"

"Very. We've got enough time to shower and get to the office." Organised and buttoned-up Mitchell was firmly in charge again.

They walked down the street. Whip knew the neighbourhood pretty well, having spent a few years in the city when he'd attended the Eugene Lang College of Liberal Arts. He'd loved New York but his involvement in superpowers had steered his life in a different direction.

He'd had a bizarre encounter one night in the subway right underneath Canal. A weird, troll-like man had approached him and said, "The time has come."

Creepy, homeless people were not uncommon in New York, except the man had known Whip's name and added, "Your grandpa, Otis, has left you his legacy. You have to come with me."

Oh, joy. Whip had been on his way uptown to see a play. He didn't have time to discuss legacies, but he'd been quickly surrounded by a bunch of small folk and was surprised to learn he'd been approached by an actual, real-life troll. He really hadn't thought they existed.

Whip knew better now, since he was the master of their domain. He had inherited the mantle of Earth Mage and had been required to sit on the jury of several superpower court cases.

Being an Earth Mage had its charms and its...disadvantages. He'd learned why he was attracted to certain men. All of them, he realised, were Earth signs of the Zodiac. Though Whip enjoyed sex — enjoyed it a lot, actually — he found it easier to keep his distance and have frequent booty calls. It meant that he didn't have to explain why he showed up in bed covered in mud late at night...and why arguing trolls sometimes appeared in the kitchen.

Trolls, he'd learned, liked to argue a lot. Whip had discovered that there were secret underground cage fights going on and a lot of young men had been killed. Some of them had been thrown into the ring stoned, or forced to perform due to debts they owed. They'd disappeared, their heartsick families never knowing their fate.

Whip had stepped in and created mud fights, hoping that channelling the aggression into more regulated events would help avoid some of the problems. He knew earth-bound folk loved mud and Whip ensured all participants were willing. He'd taken the idea to World Wide Wrestlers, Inc., giving the project legitimacy. Still, Whip found that he had to participate sometimes in unofficial fights. Being given the privilege of being a wrestling superstar, he'd acquiesced to the Earth Council's edict that he take part in the occasional 'underground' fight, with the income from ticket sales being distributed for charitable purposes. He'd finally agreed, although lately those underground fights seemed to happen more and more.

What had Mitchell said to him? '*You're all work and no play.*' That wasn't far from the truth. He stopped suddenly. Where the hell were they?

Mitchell looked white. He stared up at a street sign. His voice trembled. "Why did you bring us here?"

"I didn't."

Whip looked around. His daydreaming had led them way off course. They'd never make it in time to take a shower *and* get to the meeting now. Mitchell was upset and he knew it had nothing to do with being off course. Whip glanced at the sign. *Marley Place*. Mitchell looked like he'd seen a ghost. Hmm…perhaps he had.

"You used to live here?" Whip kept his tone soft. Mitchell's defences shut down immediately. He looked bewildered as he turned to gaze at Whip.

"How did you know?"

Whip shrugged. "Want to check it out?"

Mitchell hesitated. Oh man, the guy was really upset. Bad memories were associated with this street. He propelled Mitchell forwards, putting a hand under his elbow.

At number ten, Mitchell stopped. A doorman who looked well past retirement age let a woman out of the attractive apartment building. He closed the door firmly, giving Whip and Mitchell a distrustful look.

"I used to live here," Mitchell blurted. Whip was surprised Mitchell was being so direct, but that was a quality that had impressed him the first time they'd spoken. Whip glanced up at the building's faux-stone exterior. It had an art-deco appearance with gargoyles perched on the corners. He wondered if they had been scary to a little kid.

"When?" the doorman asked. "I've worked here for twenty years. You're not familiar to me."

"I was a lot younger then." Mitchell's wry smile seemed to get to the doorman.

"Who were your parents?" he asked.

Mitchell didn't respond. Whip read his mind now. *Kathy and Louie Dykins*. But he couldn't say it. Mitchell would fall apart.

"Kathy and Louie Dykins."

The doorman's facial expression changed. "My God...you're Louie's kid? I shoulda recognised you." He jumped forwards and hugged Mitchell. To Whip's astonishment, both men wept.

"I loved your father," the doorman said, turning away again, reaching for a handkerchief from his pocket and blowing his nose loudly.

Mitchell pawed at his face. "Yeah...me too."

"It all changed after he was killed, didn't it?" the doorman asked. "He was a real gentleman."

Mitchell didn't respond. He seemed to be in serious torment.

"I'm sorry about your daddy, Mitchell."

Mitchell nodded. The doorman had his hand on Mitchell's shoulder. Whip wanted to step forwards, put his arms around Mitchell and lead him to emotional safety, but he couldn't. He was riveted by the conversation.

"Thanks," Mitchell said, sounding better.

"What happened to your sister...Ashley, wasn't it?"

"Alicia."

"Alicia. Right."

"She's fine. She's in a wheelchair. But she survived."

The doorman looked woebegone. "And Kathy?"

"Kathy died two years ago."

"No, son. Kathy died the day she strapped you and your sister into the back seat of her car and ran down your father."

Mitchell gasped. Whip almost keeled over. *Holy shit.* How had Mitchell survived such a harrowing experience?

"We should go," Mitchell said. "But...I have a question. Are there still gargoyles in the lobby?"

The doorman grinned. "Yes, there are."

"Can you let Mitchell inside to see them?" Whip felt this was important. He didn't know why.

"Sure," the doorman said. "You're Mudshark Jackson, aren't you? My grandson loves you."

Mitchell grinned. "Now I feel really stupid that I didn't recognise you on the plane."

Whip posed for a photo with the man as Mitchell dutifully snapped the shot with the doorman's phone, then the three of them walked inside.

Mitchell seemed very calm as he gazed around at the hideous creatures. "They terrified the pants off me when I lived here. Now I realise they're pretty awesome."

Outside, Mitchell and the doorman hugged again.

"You know, it's weird," the elderly man said. "I usually only work on Sundays... I'm filling in for someone. What a coincidence!"

Not a coincidence. Whip knew some kind of superpower shenanigans were afoot and became more concerned than ever for Mitchell. He was in the grip of something, Whip just didn't know what. He shook the doorman's hand and put his arm around Mitchell's shoulders, steering him away. At the corner of the street, the taxi Whip had mentally summoned turned up.

"You still want to grab that shower?" he asked Mitchell.

"Yeah. You?"

"Absolutely."

They made it to the hotel in pretty good time, checked in and went to the suite that World Wide Wrestlers, Inc. had booked for him. It had a balcony overlooking 57th Street. Mitchell stood at the glass doors, looking outside.

Whip had so many questions. He just didn't want to tip the man's mental state over the edge.

"You want first shower?" he asked.

Mitchell grinned. "I'll be quick."

He was as good as his word. Whip glimpsed the guy through the half-open bathroom door and wasn't surprised to see a very nice body had been concealed underneath the form-hiding clothes. He also had a nice, big, juicy-looking cock.

"Here, why don't you put these on?"

As Mitchell came out with a towel around his waist, Whip tossed him a pair of his trademark white underpants with a hand grenade painted on the crotch. The manufacturers gave Whip fresh samples every week. Mitchell stared at the clear package, his face aglow.

"Really?"

Whip laughed. He was beginning to like this guy. He raced into the bathroom, liking the strong scent of Mitchell's earthy body shampoo.

"Mind if I use your body wash?" he called out.

"Help yourself," Mitchell called back. Oh man, he looked hot in those tighty-whities. Whip found his cock hardening as he glanced at that cute ass. He licked his lips. In the shower, he stroked himself in a half-hearted way. He actually enjoyed prolonging his arousal and had found he kept a clearer mind if his body was not fully sated. He increased the cold water flow, imagining he was fucking Mitchell's nice, tight ass, and soaped up with the Perry Ellis shower gel. It was right up Whip's alley. So was Mitchell.

He stepped out of the shower, dried off and changed in the room, letting Mitchell get an eyeful of him as he stepped into a pair of his own grenade underpants.

Mitchell looked up at him. "You are the hottest man I've ever seen."

"Thanks." Whip dressed quickly. "You ready?"

Mitchell got to his feet. As he joined him in the hallway, Whip put his hand on the back of Mitchell's neck. He didn't know why, but he liked touching the guy. He almost kissed him. There was some confused sexual tension between them, but Whip looked forward to straightening things out later. Alone. Together. In bed.

They grabbed a taxi outside and made it to the meeting with minutes to spare.

The office staff all grovelled over Whip. Whip knew that Lucy, the secretary, had the hots for him. She'd sent him several provocative emails and left a few suggestive voicemail messages. His wall of silence must have triggered her 'clue' button because she was polite, but nervous, and he made sure not to hug her or engage in any of the friendly, flirty things he used to.

Lucy did sit next to him, however — leaning into him as often as possible as she took notes. She was beginning to bug him. Across the table, he watched Mitchell masterfully handle his PowerPoint presentation, passing the sample trading cards around the table. Lucy spent a long time studying Mudshark's card.

Larry Parker, owner of the company, ran in late with his newest bimbo du jour. She wore a cowboy hat, slip dress and cowboy boots. She had the vibe of a porn star and the frozen smile of those tiny terrors on *Toddlers and Tiaras*. Whip instinctively disliked her.

"I'm sorry, I'm sorry," Parker said, flapping his hands as if shooing away flies. "Start again, Mitchell. And where are those damned cards?"

Mitchell went through it all again, Lucy staring daggers at Larry's girlfriend. Mitchell was such an entertaining presenter that Whip was certain he was the only one to catch Larry's girlfriend poking her tongue out at Lucy.

Lucy gasped and Mitchell stopped speaking.

"Anything wrong?" he asked Lucy.

"No, no." Lucy looked devastated. She may have been on the verge of saying something except that Larry spoke up. He was an odd, skinny duck with a bad toupee and teeth that didn't fit. He reminded Whip of a young Don Knotts, without the sense of humour.

"We have a problem," Larry said. Whip sat up straighter.

"Problem?" he and Mitchell said in unison.

"Jerry Jones has pulled out of WWW. He's got a legal problem he needs to take care of and he's worried that public exposure will only add to his hassles. We're gonna need to replace him."

A groan went around the table. Everybody knew how difficult it had been getting the crew they had now.

"I have an idea," Whip said. All eyes turned to him. "Let's give Mitchell his card. He can be the new Mudpit Madman. It can be an honorary card. He doesn't have to go into the ring but considering he's at every fight, I think the fans would love having a team member who's part of the geek squad."

Mitchell laughed. "If I wasn't a geek, I'd be offended."

Everybody started talking at once. They loved the idea. Larry Parker banged the table so hard he rattled his own teeth. They flew across the table and landed in front of Lucy.

"Ooopth," Larry said. "My new implanths are sthill on back order."

Lucy reached for a napkin with some dignity, wrapped the dentures and slid them back to him. Larry took them out, dunked them in his glass of mineral water and sloughed them back into his mouth.

Eeewww!

Meeting over, Mitchell and Whip left the offices together.

"Thanks for suggesting me for a card," Mitchell said.

"No problem. You've worked so hard. You deserve it." He punched the elevator button.

"What time is your fight tonight?"

Whip had forgotten he was performing at Madison Square Garden. He'd booked so many appointments — to get his hair trimmed, a photo shoot, and...

They stepped into the elevator and the damned thing dropped. The doors hadn't even closed yet when the elevator plummeted, sending Whip and Mitchell falling towards ground level, driving Whip's stomach up into his throat.

Whip almost went over the edge before Mitchell pulled him back in.

"We're gonna die!" Mitchell crawled to his feet. "Oh, God. My sister's gonna be all alone!"

"Relax. We're not going to die." Whip sat up now, wondering how he could explain to Mitchell his alter ego's existence in the secret superpower realm.

"We're not?"

Whip got to his knees and grabbed Mitchell's face. He kissed the guy. Mitchell's eyes widened but he got over his shock and kissed him back. Damn, it was nice. Whip wished he could have taken things a step further right here in the elevator, except they'd just arrived.

In Middle Earth.

He could hear the fans chanting. "Mudshark, Mudshark!"

"What the..." Mitchell's words fell away.

"It's a mud fight. A real mud fight." Whip stood and helped Mitchell to his feet. He put his hand on the back of the man's neck as they moved forwards into the darkness. Beyond the elevator, he could see the bright lights of the mudpit. Whip wondered what Mitchell made of the gladiator-style arena. He looked stunned but hadn't started screaming yet.

"Your opponent failed to show up," the MC came and told Whip. A smarmy, dark-haired guy in a suit, he was, however, a great fight host.

"Who's this? You brought your own opponent?" The MC looked ecstatic. "Guys, guys! Whip's brought a new victim...er...I mean, challenger."

"No, he hasn't!" Mitchell squawked, but it was too late. The trolls had emerged and dragged Mitchell off to change.

"Help!" Mitchell screamed.

"Don't worry." Whip was right behind him. "I won't hurt you. I'll pretend to smack you a couple of times and you should just go down. Okay?"

Mitchell gulped, staring back over his shoulder at Whip.

"You said it was an honorary card. Holy shit. Look at these people!"

The trolls had stripped Mitchell down to his underwear…the underwear Whip had given him.

"Blasphemy!" the fans roared, throwing handfuls of mud at Mitchell.

Whip stripped off quickly and stepped into the pit. The fans screamed. Mitchell, after getting over his initial shock, seemed to get into the spirit of things, giving the fans the finger. He turned around and faced Whip, wild laughter on his lips.

"What was in my coffee?" he yelled.

He let Whip take control at the opening bell, allowing Whip to pretend-punch him. However, the crowd's laughter seemed to get to him and he started fighting back. Mud will do that to a guy. Whip became turned on. He fell on top of Mitchell at one point, their cocks rubbing against one another in the mud.

They traded heated glances. Fuck…they were so hot for each other. Mitchell overpowered Whip and climbed on top of him. The crowd went mad as Mitchell straddled him and held up his hands in victory.

Whip began to panic. He had a ten count before Mitchell was declared the victor.

"One, two, three…" the troll counted.

The referee troll appeared out of nowhere.

Mitchell didn't seem to be aware they were in a fight. He rubbed his hands over Whip's body, his eyes darkening with excitement and arousal. Mitchell seemed intent on ravishing Whip right there. As much as he might like that, this was so not the place and time.

Whip almost screamed when the troll kept counting, reminding him of reality and his current predicament.

"…four, five, six…!"

"Mudshark!" the crowd screamed.

Then out of a distant corner, a new chant began. "Madman! Madman!"

"…seven, eight…!"

And Whip fought for the first time in a long time. Muscles straining, he attempted to overpower a still-grinning Mitchell. It wasn't easy to try to throw off the hottest man he'd come across in what seemed like forever, but he had to try. He desired the man atop him, but he couldn't let a geek overpower him. Nothing less than his career and reputation were at stake here.

"…nine, ten! Seconds out!"

Holy crap. Whip had just lost his first fight. Ever.

He closed his eyes and the world began to spin. He opened his eyes again and found himself on his back in their hotel room, covered in mud, his raging cock spilling out of the side of his underpants. Mitchell still sat astride him, panting. His cock, too, was rigid.

Whip didn't know whether to fight the man or fuck him.

"What the fuck…?" Mitchell managed, his shocked gaze going everywhere.

"I can explain," Whip said. "I think."

Chapter Three

"You *think* you can explain?" Mitchell wasn't sure he wanted to know. The weirdness of the past few hours was getting to him. He glanced around again, just to make sure that what he'd seen was real. As far as he was able to judge they were back in Whip's hotel room, and the sun was just about to set. They had brought some mud with them, which was more than a little worrying, but he was willing to overlook that fact for a while longer.

"Yeah." Whip frowned and took a breath, as if ready to speak.

"Can it wait?" He had a far more urgent issue. The raging hard-on he'd developed during the fight — had that really been him? — wouldn't go away.

He wanted to rub himself against Whip until they both came. He had one of the most amazing wrestlers on his back, underneath him. Not something he'd ever thought would happen to him, and he needed to take advantage of it while it lasted. The equally hard erection against his own throbbing cock confirmed that Whip was into this as much as Mitchell. As

44

absurd as the situation was, knowing Whip was with him gave him the courage to act on his quickly increasing arousal.

"Wait?" Whip's eyebrows rose and he wriggled, trying to free himself.

"Yeah, wait." Mitchell bent down, close enough to bring their chests into contact as he supported himself on his hands. He licked a path up Whip's neck, loving the salty sweetness of Whip's sweat. It had an earthy, musky flavour and was totally addictive. When he reached Whip's earlobe he couldn't resist and sucked on it.

Whip's struggle became more intense and the man started to pant as Mitchell kept up the suction. When he brought his teeth into play, Whip's hips bucked and they both groaned. The pressure on Mitchell's balls was exquisite torture and the friction of the soft fabric of his grenade underpants against his cock was maddening.

"Now you've got it." Mitchell pulled back the tiniest bit so he could look into those chocolate eyes.

"Hold on." Whip slid one hand to Mitchell's ass, the other up to his nape.

The increased force against Mitchell's groin was just what he needed. With renewed vigour he ground into the hardness beneath him, slanting his lips over Whip's for a kiss that was unrestrained and more passionate than Mitchell had thought possible.

He closed his eyes, gripped Whip's shoulders to have something to hold on to, and sank into a battle of tongues far more pleasurable than the fighting they'd done earlier. Whip gave as good as he got and Mitchell was close to coming within seconds. Whip's hand on his nape held him steady as the guy somehow managed to take control of the kiss, pushing his hot tongue into Mitchell's mouth in the same rhythm as he was moving his hips.

Conscious thought ceased as Mitchell's balls pulled up and he started chasing his orgasm. Whip circled his hips, and the added sideways movement was Mitchell's undoing. He threw back his head as his back bowed with the intensity of the ecstasy racing along his nerve endings until it exploded out of his cock. His mouth opened and he wanted to scream with how good it felt, but no sound emerged. His body shook as he came in spurt after spurt of hot release.

Whip's hips started jerking uncontrollably as he shuddered through his orgasm. But even then the trembling didn't stop. Instead, it got stronger. The bed began to shake and it felt as if the entire building was swaying. An earthquake? In New York? A strong scent of hot mud, decomposing plants and wet earth permeated the room. The light outside their window went from early dusk to midnight black and the rolling sound of underground thunder threatened to overwhelm him. After another panic-filled few seconds the weird effects subsided and things went back to normal. Well, what passed for normal since he'd met Whip.

"Fuck!" Mitchell collapsed, using his last functioning brain cell to roll to his side. He turned his head towards Whip to check if the man had noticed the strange goings-on. "Did you feel that?"

"Yes." Whip sounded more exhausted than shocked. The man dropped his head onto the pillow and put one arm over his eyes. Was he trying to hide?

"Why aren't you more upset?" He was ready to run, except he didn't know where to go. Whatever this…effect…had been, it had involved the very Earth itself. How did you escape something like that?

"Because I think it may have something to do with what happened to us before." Whip sighed and pulled back his arm so he could look at Mitchell. "Except, if I'm right, we have a real problem on our hands, rather than just a weird occurrence."

"You call being transported to some underground fighting place by a dropping elevator a 'weird occurrence'?" Mitchell turned to his side, now facing Whip.

"Because I wasn't sure what had caused it." Whip sat up, grabbed some of the convenient tissues from the nightstand and cleaned himself up before handing a few to Mitchell. He leaned against the headboard.

"And now you are?" He followed Whip's example, which didn't make him very clean, but at least the worst of the stickiness was gone. He sat cross-legged so he faced him and could watch the fighter's expressive face during what he hoped to be one hell of an explanation.

"Let's just say that I have a theory." Whip rubbed his forehead. "Let me ask you a few more questions and I promise I will tell you all I know."

"Okay." He was curious as all get-out, but what he knew about Whip made it clear that he wasn't going to divulge anything before he was good and ready.

"How close were you to your father?"

"My father?" Mitchell's heart sank. He still missed him every single day.

Whip nodded. There was more than simple curiosity in his eyes.

"He died when I was five, Whip. What do you want me to say? I was way too young to understand anything more than that he was my daddy." He blinked away the tears that came to his eyes. Shit, first they'd practically walked into his parents' home at Marley Place, somewhere he hadn't even thought about in many years, and now Whip wanted to know details he wasn't sure he could supply, even if he tried.

"I'm sorry. I didn't realise you were that young when he was killed." Whip looked away for a few seconds, clearly embarrassed. When he looked back up, his eyes were filled with compassion. "I wouldn't bring this up if it wasn't important, please believe me."

"I do believe you. That doesn't take away the fact that it's painful to even think of him, never mind talk about him." Actually, it was more the manner of his death and his mother's subsequent refusal to even acknowledge what she'd done. "Why did you bring him up?"

"Because I think that what happened today is somehow linked to your heritage. A legacy that was taken away from you by someone who is trying to interfere in Earth House matters." Mitchell frowned in confusion and Whip sighed. "And you don't have a clue what I'm talking about, do you?"

"Can't say I do." He shook his head experimentally, hoping the movement would clear the fog from his brain. No such luck.

"Okay, let me take this from the top." Whip cleared his throat. "There's no easy way to say this, so I'm just going to come out and confront you with a little-known truth. Shakespeare let one of his heroes, Hamlet, express it better than I ever could. *There are more things in heaven and earth, Horatio, than are dreamt of in your philosophy.*"

"Meaning...?" Mitchell felt the hairs at the base of his neck stand upright. The feeling of foreboding almost suffocated him.

"Meaning that there is a world outside the range of normal human perception which has existed since the beginning of time. It is the realm of elemental superpowers. Their sources are Fire, Water, Earth and Air. Certain members of the supernatural world are linked to these forces — exhibiting the special 'talents' caused by them." Whip's gaze burned into him.

"Elemental superpowers?" If Whip had pulled the very floor from underneath his feet he couldn't have felt more surprised.

"Yes. I'm a part of this world. I'm a member of the Earth House, and I sometimes participate in these underground mud fights to raise cash for charitable purposes. We didn't use to have these fights, but they seem to have become increasingly popular over the last thirty years. There's a lot of politics involved, and I've been trying to figure out why we need them at all, but haven't been successful so far." Whip tilted his head, looking at him as if trying to make sure he understood.

"How do I even know that you're not making all of this up?" Aside from the minor detail that he did remember being in a fight, and the irrefutable evidence of mud now sticking to the bed sheets, he found it hard to digest. Facts aside, he needed time to assimilate the news.

"It does explain what happened, doesn't it?" Whip sighed. "Well, at least partly. What I hadn't figured out until the earthquake we just caused was what your role is in all of this."

"Hold on — you're not just telling me that there's a whole world of superpowers out there, but that I'm a part of it? And supposedly this caused an earthquake?" If he hadn't already been seated he surely would have dropped onto his ass at this point. He wanted to laugh it all off, but Whip was too serious for this to be a joke.

"For one thing, you wouldn't have come underground with me if you didn't have some link to the superpower world. Secondly, you would have never been able to win the fight. And, thirdly, the earthquake that just happened wasn't a natural phenomenon, not with all the additional side effects it came with." Whip grinned. "It was the sign—or a side effect, if you want—of an emerging Earth Power talent."

"You're seriously telling me *I* did it?" Mitchell's eyes widened, and the uncomfortable feeling in his sinking stomach confirmed Whip meant what he said. But people's thoughts, or whatever, couldn't cause earthquakes—could they?

"*I* most certainly didn't. I outgrew this sort of thing during puberty." Whip looked insulted.

"You…caused…*earthquakes*?" When Whip didn't respond, Mitchell drew a breath. "No way." *This is too crazy to be true.*

"I expected you not to believe me. So I've come up with a way to prove that what I said is right." Whip grinned suddenly. "I want you to focus on producing another earthquake."

"What?" Mitchell blinked, trying to convince himself that he hadn't heard right. "Only a true magician, maybe a talented illusionist, could do something like that."

"Just do me a favour, and try. What have you got to lose? If it doesn't work, then you know none of this is true. But if it does, will you give me another chance to explain things to you?" Whip's pleading eyes were what did it.

Mitchell nodded. It couldn't hurt to try and do as the man said. The problem was that he didn't have a clue what to do. How did one go about causing an earthquake? Then he thought back to the feelings he'd had when he came. Their intensity had certainly beaten anything he'd ever experienced before. Trying to reproduce those wasn't going to be a hardship.

He closed his eyes for better focus and looked inward. This was a lot like meditating to try to assimilate the lost pieces of his soul. In a way, trying to find what Whip said was a missing talent was not all that dissimilar. The remembered euphoria, when it came, overwhelmed him. The softly shaking bed shocked him into opening his eyes again. He lost his concentration and everything went back to normal.

Whip wore the broadest grin on this face.

"What?" He didn't understand how this could be seen as funny in the least. "You're telling me this isn't some cheap magic trick? I'm not on Candid Camera?"

"Nope. Just to be sure, why don't you try again?" Whip lifted a hand as if to stop him from doing so right away. "And just to make sure you understand — magic and superpowers are two entirely different things. Most people wouldn't know the difference, since their effects are very similar, if not identical in some cases. But the truth is, superpowers come from within the person who wields them, magic is something learned. Anyone can study to become a magician, but you have to be born with a superpower talent — there's no way of 'learning' it."

"So what you're saying is that I was born with an ability to cause earthquakes? Why didn't I know this?" Surely he should have noticed *something* weird in the thirty years of his life?

"I think your powers were dormant. You had nobody to teach you, since your father died when you were too young for them to have surfaced. Usually, they come out when people go through puberty, at which point their parents can guide them. You never had that." Whip shrugged. "And your powers may consist of more than a talent to cause an earthquake. There are many types of superpowers linked to the Earth House — the connection to earthquakes is just the most obvious one."

Mitchell shook his head and focused on trying to make the earth shake again. He did. Several times. The evidence staring him in the face half an hour later was overwhelming.

"Shit!" What the hell was he supposed to do now?

"I'll help you, if you want." Whip's voice was soft, his deep brown eyes full of understanding.

"You would do that?"

"Sure. I was the one who drew you into this situation, even if it wasn't on purpose, so, in a way, I feel responsible. I also think your talent may be a lot stronger than we can see right now. With everything that's happened over the past thirty years, the Earth House has lost track of too many members." Whip raked his long, gleaming hair and Mitchell wanted to join him and play with it. "One of our Earth Mages is missing, for God's sake, so we're not even up to full speed as it is."

"Earth Mage?" He could feel the headache approaching with giant steps.

"Yes, they're the most powerful members of any of the four houses. Each one only has five, so, with one missing, we are weaker than we should be." Whip shrugged. "I'm hoping that you may be the missing man's successor, but I have no idea how that would be possible since your father wasn't a Mage."

This was fast becoming too much. "How do we know he wasn't?"

"Your mother killed him." Whip stared at him. "Unless you have a powerful grandpa? Sometimes it skips a generation."

"I don't know my grandparents." Mitchell was aware of the stiffness in his tone. After his father died and his mom went bonkers, a lot of people in their lives just...disappeared.

"Interesting." Whip seemed to be considering things. "We might need to look up your old cheese."

My old cheese? Mitchell loved this expression for older family members. He shook his head. He hadn't slept much last night, the work day had been long and tiring, and the strange underground fight had definitely taken it out of him.

"Who is this missing Mage?" he asked.

"Long story and I will explain it to you. There's a lot of pieces to it. We won't solve that part of the riddle now, though. You look as tired as I feel, so how about we catch some sleep?" Whip held out his hand while silently pointing at the bathroom with the other. "I have the Madison Square Garden fight later tonight, so I'll just take a short nap. But you don't have to go — you can stay here and catch up on all your missing sleep."

And miss watching Whip perform? Not on my life!

* * * *

Mitchell was glad they'd taken the time to shower before they dressed and left for Whip's fight. Whip seemed withdrawn, which made sense since he was mentally preparing himself for his match. They walked some of the way to the venue and, though Mitchell was sweat-soaked by the time they grabbed a taxi, it was better than having itchy, leftover come and mud sticking to him as well as his clothes. August in New York was way too humid for his liking.

Whip had the cab driver drop them off at the front door of the imposing building then banged the car door shut and vanished around a corner. Mitchell felt inexplicably bereft and couldn't wait to be reunited with Whip after the fight. Their own mud fight and subsequent sexual encounter had been unexpected, but totally delicious. Mitchell could easily get addicted to having Whip around, even though he knew it would probably be over once he returned home. He wasn't even sure where Whip lived. Not that it was relevant since the man travelled all over the country for his work.

His first priority was to find a World Wide Wrestlers, Inc. representative to check if there was any company seating available. The large numbers of people already lining up to get in were overwhelming and more than a little scary in how determined they were to make it inside first, even though it was still over an hour before the fight.

He noticed a scalper out front selling VIP plastic-laminated credentials at three grand a pop. *Wow*. Mitchell stopped and checked. To his dismay, the credential was his own! He gaped, wondering how the hell his name had come to appear there. Several people named Mitchell Dykins were already shuffling through the security line.

Mitchell called his boss from his cell phone. Larry Parker went berserk. Seconds later, he came hurtling out of the main entrance, his furious, beady gaze fixed on the scalper.

"Harry! You fucking bastard!" he shrieked. Harry — now that Mitchell thought about it — looked a lot like Larry Parker.

"How can you fucking do this to me?" Larry threw himself at Harry and they slapped at each other like prom queens, until a security guard showed up, looking nervous.

"Aren't you going to do something?" Mitchell asked the guy whose gaze shifted from left to right. Mitchell's own anger bubbled to the surface. He felt a rumble beneath his feet.

"Earthquake!" people shouted, but this being New York, nobody was going to allow a natural disaster to prevent them from getting into the wrestling match.

Mitchell worked hard to stop the ground shaking. He had to learn to keep his emotions in check.

"How many of these have you sold?" Larry screamed at Harry who adjusted the hairpiece on his shiny scalp.

"About thirty," he mumbled.

"Fucking liar!" Larry kicked Harry in the shin.

"All right, all right! Three hundred!"

Three hundred? Mitchell swallowed hard. Three hundred people pretending to be him were now circling the sports arena inside the fabled complex.

"My brother is such an ass." Larry snatched the remaining credentials from Harry, propelling Mitchell inside. "How did he get hold of your credential card, anyway?"

Mitchell had no clue. He'd been so busy rocking the world, his own and that around him, that he hadn't been on top of things all day. Neglecting his professional responsibilities wasn't like him...at all.

Larry escorted him into the arena to one of the press tables and took off to deal with another calamity. Mitchell could see the fans wearing their favourite wrestlers' costumes—among them, Mudshark's grenade underpants. Nobody looked as good as Whip did.

I had sex with him!

Mitchell felt weird as he took a seat beside a reporter from a boxing website. The guy gave him an odd look. On top of that, Mitchell had the odd feeling that someone else was watching him. Turning around surreptitiously didn't help him reveal who it might be, and it wasn't a good sensation. Despite his miraculous win over Whip in the strange underground arena, he was no fighter and had no idea how to defend himself should it become necessary. But who would be after him in the first place?

He shook it off as a case of overwrought nerves. Next thing he knew, he was being yanked to his feet by a security guard.

"Another Mitchell Dykins!" The guard dragged him away and would have tossed him out on the street had Mitchell not shown him his driver's licence.

Unfortunately, he couldn't get back to the press table and couldn't reach Larry. *Damn.* He made his way towards the information booth to ask for help.

"You say you work for World Wide Wrestlers Inc.?" The lady with the fluffy blonde hair, who guarded the booth and her VIP list, looked him up and down, clearly sceptical. "I've never even seen you here before."

"I'm their new marketing manager." Mitchell knew he didn't look like a wrestler—why did she have to embarrass him by looking at him as if he'd crawled out from under a rock?

"Aha, that explains it." With a sardonic little half-grin, as if happy she'd won a bet against herself, she picked up the phone to call his boss and verify his identity.

"Oh, hello, Mr. Parker. It's Jackie from the reception hall booth here." She smiled, fiddled with her hair, as if anyone cared, and finally turned away from Mitchell to create more privacy.

Mitchell rolled his eyes as he watched her listen to Larry's response.

"Well, I have this…gentleman…here who says he's your new marketing manager." She tilted her head. "I thought I better check with you to make sure he's legit. You know, because of the new security protocols and everything."

Mitchell shook his head. She should have been a security guard.

"Mitchell Dykins." She paused to listen to more instructions then nodded. "Thank you so much, and I'm sorry to have bothered you."

She turned around and forced a smile on her lips.

"You're good to go." She put down the receiver. "Section two hundred, row G. I'll give you a ticket."

"Wait…I was in the press row before."

She gave him a baleful stare and handed him his ticket. He took it, thanked her and ran.

"There you are." Larry beamed at him. "It's better you sit here with us." Mitchell didn't really care, though he should have had the opportunity to mingle with the media. He kept a smile on his face as his boss introduced him to two of his colleagues, both avid wrestling fans who expressed their gratitude several times within the next few minutes for the opportunity to watch a live match.

Mitchell tuned out their voices and looked around. He had a great view of the ring. Not quite front and centre, but close enough. That, he decided as he watched the mud being spread liberally across the slightly modified floor, was probably a good thing. There was a small protective ridge around the ring's edge, but it wasn't high enough to stop the muddy sludge from flying when one of the performers was dropped or thrown onto the floor. Anyone in the first few rows was likely to be covered in the stuff within the first few minutes of the fight.

On huge TV screens above the arena, the dressing room action came to life. A camera crew visited the wrestlers as they prepared for battle. Mudshark wore a white terrycloth robe as he instructed his teammates on the meaning of victory.

God, he is hot... Mitchell felt his cock stirring in his pants as the crowd went nuts at the mere sight of Whip Jackson.

"This battle tonight is bigger than any fight...ever!" he said, punching his closed right fist into his left hand. "This one is for all the marbles...which is why I won't tolerate any losers."

Wow...he does sound like a bit of an...ass.

The scene cut to Mudshark's opponent, a giant by the name of Emir 'The Snake' Putin. He was massive. He was a new member of the stable of fighters Mitchell's company represented, which was scary. The guy had a seriously deranged look to his eyes. With dark skin, gleaming black hair and a scowl worthy of some kind of Guinness World Record, he stomped around his dressing room.

As the TV screens turned blank and the arena went black, the crowd began to roar its appreciation. Mitchell had a sense of what it must have been like back in the days of Christians in the lions' den...of gladiators...

The lights went up so brightly, the arena looked like Christmas. On the screen, a tunnel became illuminated as The Snake marched into the arena, accompanied by his posse, all decked out in faux snakeskin capes.

Some of the crowd cheered The Snake as he strode into the ring, taking up residence in the corner kitted out with a snakeskin-covered stool. At least Mitchell hoped it wasn't the real thing. He had no particular love for snakes, but no creature deserved to be skinned only to end up as a decoration in a mock fight. The Snake's muscles bulged as he sat down, pretending not to worry about the upcoming fight.

Whip entered next and Mitchell's mouth watered. He may not have been as massive as his opponent, but he was beautiful. Every muscle was well sculpted, not a hair out of place, and the trademark white fighting pants with the hand grenade in a very strategic position drew Mitchell's eyes like they had from the very first Mudshark fight he'd ever watched. He had no idea what the planned outcome for this match was, only sure that it had been scripted like all professional wrestling games, but he knew he was going to enjoy watching Mudshark give his all.

Once the referee had taken up his position, the announcer's voice rang out.

"Welcome, ladies and gentlemen." The booming voice made people sit up and pay attention, quieting down the crowd immediately. "We're happy to see you here tonight for our double billing. I'll tell you more about the second event after the break, but first we have a contest between two giants of the World Wide Wrestlers' group of veteran fighters for you. Emir 'The Snake' Putin versus Whip 'Mudshark'

Jackson will show you what two mud fighters can do when we let 'em loose!"

The crowd roared its approval.

"The contest is set for three falls with a half-hour time limit." The announcer chuckled. "And what a half hour it will be to watch, since I am sure neither of these warriors will go down easily."

More applause. The opponents took their positions. The Snake made sure to stomp along the edge, making the first bits of mud fly out of the ring. A few worried glances from the people sitting in the first few rows made Mitchell smile. They were beginning to realise what they might be in for.

The first minutes were spent with both fighters circling each other, kicking as much mud as possible outside the ring, covering the floor as well as a few spectators in the brown stuff. Mitchell guessed that the less remained, the easier it would be for them to. fight.

Emir lost his patience first and lunged for Mudshark headlong. Mudshark used his superior agility to evade him and countered by bending down to pick up some mud to decorate The Snake's face with.

The crowd loved it.

The Snake yelled, clawed at his face to wipe off the mud and managed to catch Mudshark in a tight clinch. Muscles straining, both fighters breathed more deeply and the crowd held its collective breath. Mudshark slowly lost ground until The Snake toppled him, winning the first fall.

Mudshark made a fast recovery. He mimed taking his gloves off and throwing them into the crowd, who lapped it up. The Snake was distracted long enough to miss the full-body slam that landed him on his ass, spattering mud everywhere.

One lady in a pink dress let loose a high-pitched scream, jumped up and left the hall in a huff. The man in the seat next to her now empty one grinned, shrugged and turned his attention back to the fight.

Mudshark got a tight grip of The Snake and manoeuvred him into a corner, using the backlash of the ropes to catapult them both across half the ring where he stopped, let go of The Snake and let the guy's momentum crash him into the ropes on the other side. The force of the backlash threw a howling Snake on his ass in the middle of the mud puddle for the second time.

Mitchell began to be excited. Only one more fall and Mudshark would win the fight. Thoughts of a possible celebration distracted him into missing The Snake's next move, which resulted in Mudshark getting pinned to the ground without a hope of escape.

Shit!

A ten-count by the referee later, both opponents jumped up. It was now two-two and Mudshark only needed one more fall to win the game.

Mitchell squirmed in his seat. He knew these fights were just for show, for entertainment. The problem was that they seemed so real. He was rooting for Mudshark, as he always did, and hoped he'd win as he always had so far...except for that one fluke in the underground fight. But that didn't really count, did it? It was an entirely different realm — one of superpowers, if Whip was right. Would it influence what happened here?

Mitchell turned his attention back to the fight. Both opponents were circling each other again, occasionally grappling and attempting to throw each other.

"Come on, Whip, come on!" Mitchell had a hard time to remain seated.

Three seats down his boss was far too relaxed for Mitchell's liking. Larry had probably cheated and checked the script. Mitchell was going to suffer through every up and down. Right now, there was a lot of mud-slinging going on, covering more spectators in brown goo. Most took it in stride, but there were a few annoyed faces as well.

One was directly opposite. His eyes were attempting to burn holes into Mitchell. What was the man's problem? Why was he watching Mitchell and not the fight? Mitchell looked more closely and gasped. With shoulder-length and straggly black hair, a pronounced three-day growth, broad shoulders, the man looked a lot like Whip's image on the trading card Mitchell had created. But that was impossible. Right?

Mitchell shook his head and looked again, only to find that the man was gone. Disconcertingly, the chair was now empty rather than occupied by another spectator. That was too weird. Still, he was probably just seeing things.

Just then, a roar went up in the audience. Mitchell looked back into the ring and watched Mudshark apply a chokehold to a kneeling Snake. He was going to try to win via making his opponent submit. That was a risky move in a high-stakes game, since the possibility of an escape was higher than with a throw. But the crowd clearly loved it and cheered Mudshark on.

Inch by inch The Snake subsided, sliding lower in the mud. Mudshark didn't let go, no matter what the other guy tried. Finally, light blue in the face, The Snake hit the ground in a gesture of surrender.

"Yes!" Mitchell jumped up and cheered with the rest of the crowd. When he sank back into his seat, he sighed with contentment. "That was amazing."

"Quite entertaining," Larry agreed, almost looking bored.

Well, that's what you get for cheating. Takes all the fun out of a fight performance like this. Mitchell shook his head, suddenly thirsty. He'd need to get something to drink before making his way to the performers' area to attempt to get in so he could congratulate Whip. They hadn't had the time to agree where to meet up after the fight, but Mitchell assumed they'd manage somehow. He was in an extremely good mood and fired up for more action with Whip...in bed, he hoped. The man was too delicious to resist and he wanted to share a lot more with him than simple frottage, as nice as it had been.

He made his way to the closest bar, but got distracted by the sign for the men's room. Definitely a good idea.

He pushed open the door and entered the oddly gloomy space. Not two steps into the half-darkness someone gripped his upper arm, pulled him against a well-muscled chest into a stranglehold and smashed the outside door closed.

"Got you!" The deep voice sounded awfully familiar, yet somehow off. "It's about time you met your just reward! And don't think I'll go easy on you."

Chapter Four

Mitchell automatically lifted his one available hand, the other being pinned by the guy's second arm around his middle, immobilising him. He tried to dislodge the arm around his throat to stop this man from strangling him. Thick muscles bulged, and his hand slid off without any effect. He tried scratching next then brought his feet into play, trying to kick the immovable giant.

Nothing helped.

The noose around his neck tightened by the second. His vision narrowed. Black nothingness threatened on the edges. A few stars appeared before his inner eye. Regret that he'd never see Whip again flooded his quickly waning conscious mind. He should have taken those self-defence classes. His uncle George appeared briefly, a sad smile on his lips. What was that all about?

With no fight left in him he slumped, ready to give in to the inevitable. Suddenly the door swung open with enough force to hit the wall behind it.

This must be a dream.

None other than Whip stood before him, his face contorted in an angry mask. He was wearing sweats and looked slightly winded, as well he should be after his fight. Little flecks of mud were still sticking to his hair and hands. His eyes widened as his gaze slid across the guy behind Mitchell and recognition made him blink. His eyes narrowed as determination hardened his features.

"Let him go, you bastard." Whip stepped closer.

"Never." The voice behind Mitchell sounded determined and the arm around his throat didn't move an inch. "You want this as much as I do."

"What?" Whip lifted his fist and advanced towards Mitchell's attacker. "I don't want Mitchell harmed. Whatever gave you that idea?"

Get on with it. Not much air left here.

"I know what you *really* want." The would-be murderer took a backwards step, dragging Mitchell with him.

God, that hurts.

"No, you don't have a clue." Whip advanced, keeping his hand up in the air, a clear threat for the attacker to see. "If you don't let Mitchell go right now, you'll regret it."

"Make me." The attacker stopped abruptly as if he'd run into a wall. A slight loosening of his hold around Mitchell's neck enabled him to take a quick, rasping breath before the pressure on his windpipe was back as strong as before.

Whip didn't speak. Instead, his eyes began to glow as he reached for the attacker. As soon as he touched the man's skin, there was a gurgling sound, and the pressure on Mitchell's throat was gone. He heaved a breath and slid sideways, out of the suddenly powerless man's grip. The scent of burning earth rose in Mitchell's nose as he turned around to look at his would-be assassin.

"Shit!" Mitchell's jaw dropped.

The attacker looked exactly like Mudshark on the trading cards, and the man he'd seen across the ring earlier this evening. He started to fade, as if he was melting into the floor as he shrank. Whip kept touching and staring at him until he was completely gone.

"What the hell?" Mitchell turned towards Whip.

"Just give me...a minute." Whip stumbled and Mitchell grabbed his arm to keep him upright and help him lean against the wall of the now empty men's room.

A few deep breaths later Whip seemed okay. He stood up straight and visually examined Mitchell.

"Are you okay?" Whip's voice sounded tired.

"I am now." Mitchell took his hand and squeezed. "But I need to know what is going on here. Why was that guy trying to kill me? And why did he look like you? I mean, your trading-card personality? That was just spooky. How did you know I was in trouble in the first place? And how did you make him vanish by making him melt into the ground like that?"

"Those are all good questions. I promise I will answer them all, but not here. We're too exposed in case he comes back." Whip pulled himself together and started walking towards the door. "Let's get back to the hotel, and I'll try to explain."

"All right." His stomach suddenly came to life and reminded him that he hadn't eaten since before the business meeting.

"We'll get room service." Whip grinned as he led Mitchell outside. "And I need a shower like you wouldn't believe."

The corridors were empty. The second performance must be well on its way by now judging by the foot-stomping and cheering that echoed throughout the building. Shit, they'd been cooped up in that restroom for longer than he'd thought. Why had nobody else walked in? Surely there were more people in need of the facilities during a performance break?

The Garden Arena seemed deserted. Apart from some security people, kiosk attendants and a few fans purchasing souvenirs from the night's wrestling match, Whip and Mitchell were the only ones who seemed to be in a hurry to leave.

Whip ducked his head as if not wanting to be recognised. Mitchell understood why as a few fans turned and stared at them. Whip hurried on, Mitchell following Whip into the cab. Neither man said a word. Whip sat with his head back against the carpeted back seat of the curry-scented taxi. Their driver wore a turban it was hard to see around and seemed to be grooving to some inaudible song. It capped off what was so far a weird but wonderful day.

Mitchell was surprised to see how pale Whip looked as he leant forwards to pay the driver. He seemed exhausted as they left the taxi and took the elevator up to their hotel room. Before he could open his mouth, Whip pressed the room service menu into his hands.

"Make a choice and we'll order." Whip took off his sweatshirt and scratched his chest. Tiny bits of dried mud went everywhere. "Shit!"

Whip raced into the bathroom, stood in the tub and really started scratching. What a sight. Mitchell's stomach didn't agree and made him turn his attention back to the menu. The steak looked good, as did the baked potatoes.

"Do you know what you want?" Mitchell peeked into the bathroom, noticing that Whip had taken off his pants as well. The sight of his muscled back and tempting ass globes made Mitchell drool. He so wanted to get his hands on all that gloriously naked skin.

"Steak and potatoes is fine. Maybe some garlic bread as a starter. Oh, and mudpie for dessert, if they have it. I could live off the stuff." Whip turned on the water, stepping back to wait for it to heat up.

Mitchell made the order for their food in record time, hanging up quickly so he could run into the bathroom to join Whip. He tore off his clothes as he was staring at the rivulets of water travelling from Whip's shoulders, down his back and across his ass cheeks. He envied the few that made it into the tempting crack. He wanted to follow them with his lips and lick everywhere he could reach.

"Are you going to join me or are you just going to stand there looking decorative?" Whip's grin was infectious.

"J-join…" He shook his head at his inability to form a complete sentence and climbed into the tub.

"Hmmm, much better." Whip opened his arms and pulled Mitchell close.

Touching chest to chest had been good before, but doing it while they were both wet was delicious. He nuzzled into Whip's neck, detecting the last traces of sweat. Even that smelt divine.

"Sorry, I didn't have time for my normal after-performance shower." Whip sidled closer and slid a thick thigh between Mitchell's legs, making sure they touched in all the important places. "I was in a bit of a rush to get to you."

"Yeah, about that." Mitchell wanted to forget all the mysterious goings-on and delve into the hottest shower action he had seen in his lifetime, but his curiosity won out. "How did you know I was in trouble?"

"I'm not sure." Whip tilted his head and leant back against the tile, pulling Mitchell with him so they remained close together. "It has to do with my abilities as an Earth Mage, since I can sometimes read minds."

"You...what?" Mitchell felt as if someone had pulled the proverbial rug out from under his feet.

"It's a very rare Earth Mage talent, and not widely known, so you'd best keep it to yourself." Whip grimaced. "We wouldn't want that knowledge to get into the wrong hands."

"Whoever they may be." Mitchell frowned. If Whip couldn't explain what was going on and who was behind the assassination attempt they were in deeper trouble than he'd thought. He didn't even want to consider what the implications of a mind-reading lover were, even if it was only a temporary thing. So, he focused back on the problem at hand. "But that wasn't all?"

"No, there was a strange pull that forced me towards you. I knew you were in danger, but there was also a feeling of something fundamentally out of kilter. Like an imbalance in the natural order." Whip sighed and closed his eyes for a moment. "And when I saw who had you in his clutches it became clear that we have a massive issue."

As if someone trying to kill me isn't massive enough!
Whip looked at him as if he'd heard every word.
Hell, maybe he has?
Whip grinned.
Oh, shit!

"Don't worry, I can only normally do it with very strong emotions or thoughts." Whip lifted a hand and cupped Mitchell's cheek. "And you, sweetheart, were thinking very loudly."

"Thinking loudly?" Mitchell shook his head. *Not going there.* He needed answers, not more questions, riddles and other weirdness. "Never mind, I don't want to know right now."

"Good, because I don't want to talk about it until we've got some food in our stomachs." Whip pulled him closer and slid a hand up his back to grab his nape. "Not to mention getting clean."

"Clean?" All he was interested in was touching all that naked skin and relieving the pressure in his balls.

Whip chuckled and grabbed the soap. He rubbed it all over Mitchell's back, slid it between the globes of his ass and rubbed across his hole, making Mitchell moan. Whip knelt to do Mitchell's legs then turned him around so he could get at the front. He gave special attention to Mitchell's cock and balls, lifting them to get soap underneath. Mitchell leant back against the cold tiles for support. The intense look in Whip's eyes alone was enough to drive him to the edge, but coupled with the soft caresses of his skin, it was too much.

"Gonna!" Mitchell couldn't stop thrusting into the conveniently soapy fist Whip provided under the guise of getting him clean.

He wanted to make it last, he really did. But a few strokes of his stiff cock were all that was needed to make him come. His toes curled and he shot his load, a few globs landing on Whip's upturned face. God, that looked sexy. Whip pushed his groin against Mitchell's shin and groaned as he followed him over the edge, heat splashing between them as he jerked with pleasure.

"Fuck, I needed that." Whip looked up at him, droplets of water dripping off his eyelashes. "Fighting always makes me horny as hell."

"I can see that. It was the same after we'd fought in that underground ring, wasn't it?" Mitchell laughed and held out a hand to help Whip stand up. "Can't say I mind."

"Somehow I didn't think you would." Whip grinned and quickly soaped and rinsed before switching off the water.

They dried each other with some of the fluffiest towels in existence and Mitchell was more than half hard again by the time they were done. The sight of Whip's naked body alone would have got him there, but combined with all the touching they did, there was no way he'd be able to stop another erection.

"Food and explanations first, okay?" Whip wasn't any better off, his excitement clearly showing. He rummaged in his bag and pulled out two of his trademark pairs of underwear, throwing one at Mitchell with a grin.

He had barely pulled up the briefs when there was a knock on the door.

"Food!" they both exclaimed at the same time and raced each other to the door like kids.

Whip got there first, tore open the door and gave the poor guy on delivery duty an eyeful of naked chest. The boy swallowed visibly and his mouth opened, but no sound came out.

Mitchell raced to the closet, grabbed their robes, handed one to Whip and slipped into the other one. The guy at the door was beet red with embarrassment.

"You ordered room service?" The guy didn't look up.

"Yes, we did. Sorry about earlier." Whip stepped back. "Please put the cart next to the table, and we'll serve ourselves."

The guy nodded, did as Whip had asked and was on his way out, still not having looked up. Mitchell pulled his wallet from the discarded pants and withdrew ten dollars.

"Sorry." He handed the note to the boy before he could vanish.

"Wow, thank you." The guy glanced up quickly and smiled gratefully. "Enjoy your food."

"Thanks, we will." Whip chuckled and closed the door behind the retreating hotel employee before he returned his attention to Mitchell. "That was very generous."

"I thought he deserved a bit of compensation for the shock we gave him." Mitchell sat down at the table and reached for the silver dome covering one of the plates.

"He did." Whip sat down and uncovered the other plate. "That looks excellent."

He grabbed silverware and napkins for each of them, they put their plates on the table, added the basket with the still-warm garlic bread and dug in. The meat was tender and well seasoned, the potatoes excellent, and after a few bites he was beginning to hope that he might not starve after all.

With mudpie to follow for dessert, what could go wrong?

Watching Mitchell eat when he was clearly hungry was a revelation. Whip tried not to stare, but it was difficult. Mitchell's lips wrapped around his fork each time he pulled the food off and all Whip could think about was the man's lips wrapped around his cock. When Mitchell licked his fingers after eating some of the garlic bread, he looked at Whip from under his eyelashes and winked. The tease!

"So, you were going to explain a few things?" Mitchell was almost finished with his food and his natural curiosity came to the fore.

"Well, maybe not explain, but I have a theory about what happened." Whip pushed away his empty plate—had he really eaten that quickly?—and leant back in his chair.

"Good enough." Mitchell somehow managed to keep eating and give Whip his full attention at the same time. "So, why did a guy looking like your trading-card personality try to kill me?"

"The honest answer is that I don't know." Whip lifted a hand to stop Mitchell from interrupting. "But I think that it happened because you—or rather, your trading-card personality—defeated me in that underground ring earlier today."

"My trading-card personality?" Mitchell frowned. "But it felt like me, I mean, I remember it all as well. It wasn't as if he was a separate person or anything, like your carbon copy in that restroom."

"And that's exactly what's *really* strange about this whole mess." Whip took a deep breath. "You see, I think that something caused my trading-card personality to become a separate person. He clearly is pure Mudshark and seemed out for revenge for the defeat in the underground fight, so he attacked you to try to eliminate you as a rival. I have no idea why that should happen only to me and not to you, though."

"Why is that weird?" Mitchell tilted his head. "I mean, any weirder than the idea of split personalities who seem to be the evil part of someone running off and doing separate things?"

"I thought I had discovered the reason for all those underground fights. If all Earth people suddenly have a split personality, they could cause a lot of mayhem like that." Whip scratched his head. "Actually, maybe that is still the explanation…except, for some reason, you are an exception?"

"And if we find out what that reason is, maybe we can fix everybody else's problem?"

"It would take a miracle."

Mitchell sat up straighter and his eyes shone with enthusiasm. "So, we need the equivalent of a spiritual healer for the Earth people, right?"

"That's possible, but there is no way we can do this on our own. I mean, I may be an Earth Mage, but this is way beyond what I can do or understand." He hated admitting defeat, but this felt a lot bigger than the two of them.

"You mentioned that an Earth Mage disappeared," Mitchell reminded him. "Who was he?"

Whip's mind began to reel. How did he even begin to explain Friday Otis Doombringer to Mitchell?

"What's wrong?" Mitchell asked, concern showing in his eyes.

"Well…I don't even know what to say about him. He was a marvellous man. Wait…he is a marvellous man." Whip shook his head. "He vanished a couple of years ago and things haven't been the same in the Earth House."

"How would we even go about finding someone?"

"I have no idea. But I do know where we can go to get help." Whip smiled at the thought. He hadn't been back to the superpower-based bakery in way too long. "I think we need to go talk to Daine and Phillip."

"Who?"

Whip smiled.

"And where would that be?" Mitchell moved forwards in his seat, tension lines marring his forehead.

"Fabulous Cupcakes." He was sure Daine Paradis, the owner and a talented Fire guy, would know whom to talk to. His life partner, Phillip Sedgwick, would be able to explain the whole court case involving Friday Otis Doombringer. If not him, then Daine's business partner, Christopher Fire, a very powerful Fire Mage, would know what to do.

"Fabulous Cupcakes? You know Fabulous Cupcakes?" Mitchell's voice came out in a squeak. He sat rigid in his seat, his eyes wide with surprise.

"You know it too?" Whip asked.

"What does Fabulous Cupcakes have to do with superpowers?" Mitchell wanted to know.

"It's only the most well-liked and famous meeting place for supernaturals and their friends in all of San Francisco." It had become widely known even amongst civvies — those without superpowers — after Daine had won the Annual Cupcake Competition. It had not only earned him the well-deserved title of making the 'Best Cupcakes in San Francisco', but had enabled him to start expanding his successful business.

"Supernaturals go there?" Mitchell's eyebrows rose. "I never even noticed anything non-natural going on, and I'm in there all the time."

"I can't believe I've never seen you there. Not that I go that often — I have to watch my fighting form, you know?" Whip patted his flat stomach and Mitchell laughed. "And once I'm in there, I'm lost. I just can't resist those fluffy creations that Daine and Christopher put together."

"I know!" Mitchell licked his lips as his eyes took on a distant look. He was clearly seeing cupcakes. "I love their breakfast cupcakes, and adore the Thai lunch line they've launched. Not to mention those amazing flavoured little blancmanges they have now."

Whip's mind raced. He shook his head. It was time to see the guys at Fabulous Cupcakes, the rest of his plans and appointments in New York be damned. Solving this weirdness was far more important than sticking to plans he'd made long before he'd met Mitchell. Getting their flights changed might cause a bit of confusion, but it was preferable to sticking it out in New York with all these unsolved riddles going on.

"I like a man who knows his desserts." Whip leant forward, imagining feeding Mitchell one of the sweet morsels then licking all the crumbs off his sculpted chest and anywhere else they might have 'accidentally' fallen.

"And why does that look of yours tell me you're no longer thinking about cupcakes?" Mitchell grinned.

"What? *Moi*?" Whip couldn't suppress the laughter that bubbled up from deep inside him. "That's the most ridiculous accusation ever! Once my mind is on cupcakes, there's very little that can get me to think about something else."

"So, what did it for you this time?" Mitchell wiggled his eyebrows.

"You."

"Me?" Mitchell's cheeks flushed with happiness.

"Yeah, I was just thinking about eating you up." Whip made a mock roaring noise and lifted his hand, shaping it like a claw.

"Here, have some mudpie." Mitchell quickly handed him one of the two desserts from the cart, taking the other one for himself.

"That's not fair." Whip looked from the tempting cake with all its gooey goodness to Mitchell and back...several times. "How am I supposed to decide between the two?"

"Let me tell you a secret." Mitchell leaned closer and lowered his voice. "You don't need to make a decision. You can have your cake and eat me, too."

"Oh my God, you are so *bad*." Whip laughed out loud. "But I like it."

Mitchell's smug smile was a reward all in itself, and the little smirk stayed on his face until Whip's cell phone rang. He glanced at it and grimaced.

Phillip Sedgwick had sent him a text message.

"We have to go," Whip said.

"Go?" Mitchell licked his fingertips. "But we're just getting started."

Whip sighed. "There's an emergency meeting at the bakery." He stared hard at Mitchell. "Special subject — you."

"Me?" Mitchell looked worried. "Do they know about my earthquakes?"

Whip didn't respond at first. He was too busy throwing things into his overnight bag. "We need to hurry, sweetheart. Come on. They've arranged for special transportation."

Mitchell gaped at him then rushed around collecting his own belongings.

Whip's phone rang a second time and he took the call.

"Hey," he said, when he saw Phillip Sedgwick's name on the readout.

"Hey, yourself." He could almost see Phillip's disarming grin as he heard the man's voice. "Is Mitchell Dykins with you?"

"Yes, Mitchell's here." Whip didn't mind Phillip knowing his business.

"Good. Bring him with you."

"I intended to. What's going on?"

"Ask him."

"Ask...Mitchell?"

"Yep. Ask him about Friday."

"Friday Otis Doombringer?" Whip had no idea what was going on.

"The trolls are coming for you," Phillip said.

"Oh, no. Not the trolls." Whip regretted the words instantly. Trolls were nice...sort of. But they did smell. Whip ended the call and found Mitchell staring at him.

"Whip, did I just hear you say Friday Otis Doombringer?"

"Yes. Why?"

"How do you know him?" Mitchell's expression was odd.

"He's the missing Mage I mentioned to you."

Mitchell shook his head. "He's not missing. He's my uncle and he's alive and...um..." His gaze fell away for a moment. Whip glimpsed so much pain and suffering when Mitchell's eyes met his again. "He's living with me and my sister."

Now it was Whip's turn to stare. "Friday's okay?"

"Well...yeah." Mitchell shrugged, zipping up his bag. "Okay as he can be for a guy who has gone deaf and blind without any apparent reason."

"Deaf and blind?" Whip was furious now. "It's impossible for a Mage to have severe sensory loss, especially two essential ones."

Mitchell looked stumped. "Well, he does now."

"Since when? How? How the hell did it happen?"

Mitchell looked older all of a sudden. It occurred to Whip that the man had been handed a pretty loaded deck from childhood. Mitchell's mom killed his dad, paralysed his sister and, it appeared, he was looking after both his uncle and...what was her name? He thought back to the conversation on the street with the doorman of Mitchell's former apartments. *Alicia.* Right. His sister's name was Alicia.

"I have no idea," Mitchell said. He lapsed into silence.

Whip's mind raced. "He disappeared about two years ago. Is that when his problems started?"

"Yeah. I'd say so. It was weird. He had a fall but there was no physical injury. You're saying my uncle is your missing Mage?" Mitchell looked utterly shocked.

"Yes, I am." Whip picked up his bags as he could detect the fetid smell of trolls. They'd be here any moment. "And, from what you're telling me, it all makes sense."

"I'm glad it makes sense to you because I'm still in the dark."

"Your uncle lost his senses," Whip said.

"I just got through telling you that."

Whip took a deep breath. "What happened to your uncle was a psychic attack...a curse. From a very powerful being. I think somebody's figured out your powers have been awakened and—" Whip's voice shook with the fury he suddenly felt. "Whoever is behind this will pay, because Friday Otis Doombringer taught me everything I know."

"Say...what?" Mitchell squinted at him.

"Yeah. You heard me. He was the greatest living wrestler of all time. Ever." Whip's mind whirled into action. "Holy shit, hon. You inherited his talent!"

"I did?" Mitchell shook his head. "I don't believe it."

"Whoever did this to him is still out there." Whip heard the trolls knocking at the bathroom wall before they'd even reached it. "And whoever it is now wants to get rid of...*you*."

* * * *

Whip was fond of trolls, really he was, but he did wish the small, mud-loving creatures would just get a better grip on hygiene. Some of the welcoming committee smelt so bad it made his eyes water.

"Fuck a duck," Mitchell said when he saw the small, wild-haired men and women popping out of the walls. He sniffed the air appreciatively. "I smell tar."

Whip could have predicted that. New York's troll colonies lived in isolated pockets of roads and inside caves in Central Park. They favoured roads and highways under construction because they were impervious to noise—hence, they tended to smell like tar. Their skin absorbed it and, like most Earth House members, Mitchell would have a terrific sense of smell. Wait until he got beneath the thin veneer of the modified pitch and noticed that they smelt like poop and urine.

Yep... The sudden head jerk from his new lover told him that Mitchell could smell the dung on them now.

Why, oh why, did these handsome little folk have to roll in the stuff?

Because trolls were handsome. Their brethren, the mean and often violent purs, weren't a barrel of laughs. They were ugly and prone to biting. They also detested humans. Some trolls had secret pur blood, but as Whip cast his gaze around he glimpsed only friendly faces.

"Don't stare at their teeth," he whispered to Mitchell as he helped him climb down into the trench the trolls had dug into their elaborate underground system beneath the city streets. He moved his backpack from one shoulder to both by lengthening the straps as they moved.

"What's wrong with their teeth?" Mitchell whispered back.

"Double rows. Pointy. Bloody ugly. And they *hurt*."

Mitchell gawped as the trolls all donned dark glasses and ski masks. One of the women handed a set of each to Whip and Mitchell. Whip took a set and thanked her, Mitchell following suit.

"They can't be in sunlight. They turn to stone. And we have to leave before the next church bell chimes on the hour." Whip checked his watch.

"What happens if we don't?"

Whip looked him in the eye and tried to appear nonchalant. "They disappear."

He put his arm around Mitchell, keeping it on the small of his back, leading him over to the first illuminated hole in the wall he could find.

"They have a fantastic bullet train. It will get us to San Francisco in one hour. Just a word of warning. It smells awful." They approached a gleaming set of railway tracks, a tiny bullet sitting on one of the treads.

Mitchell squinted. "What the hell?" Mitchell looked at him. "It's a bullet."

"Yes, I know. I just told you it was a bullet train."

"But—"

The bullet suddenly expanded, a single-carriage train emerging. Large enough to uncomfortably seat two humans and a troll, steam still spurted from its metallic shell. It had, after all, made an emergency trip here.

They had forty-five seconds before the church bells started ringing. One single peal and the troll would vanish, so Whip made an executive decision and pushed Mitchell towards the gleaming bronze vehicle. He fell inside it with a sharp screech. Whip took a deep breath and followed. A bronze-blue light glimmered inside as Whip tumbled beside Mitchell, who was on his knees.

"Sorry, lover. We had to move." Whip dragged him up by the shoulders.

"Keep your arms and legs inside the vehicle at all times," their bullet's captain said. "No photos and no cell phones allowed."

"Funny fellow," Whip muttered, as he and Mitchell sat closely on the lone smooth, metallic bench. Whip reached around for his seatbelt.

"Would you prefer to walk?" the captain asked.

Whip shook his head. "No, sir."

Mitchell gagged as he fumbled for his own belt. Whip was used to trolls' really horrible breath but realised it was a new and vile experience for Mitchell.

"This is disgusting." Mitchell began to sweat. The odour was extreme, but then their captain was agitated so the smell of shit coming out of his pores inside the bullet was intense.

"Close your eyes and mouth," Whip advised. "The initial blast is horrifying. Once we push off, the smell subsides."

"If you say so."

Mitchell screamed as the carriage pulled back, launched forwards then down, plunging deep into the earth. There was nothing Whip could do to comfort the man, he was too busy hanging on for dear life himself. They hit their heads against the roof of the bullet — the sound and speed intensity was similar to a jet engine with vile odour accompanying the blast.

Whip almost passed out from the pain. He glanced at Mitchell.

Out cold. He reached out a tentative hand, hoping the man was okay...

Chapter Five

Whip pressed his fingers to Mitchell's throat, felt his pulse and relaxed. Seconds later Mitchell came to and for several, unpleasant moments Whip knew that all his senses were being assaulted by noise, putrid smells and tremors that shook him to the core. It had been the same for him the first time. As they rose back to the surface of New York's subway system, Whip tried to reassure Mitchell, who looked rigid beside him.

"Breathe!" Whip shouted over the metallic din. "We'll be okay."

"I feel like I'm in an MRI machine." Mitchell didn't look very healthy, but at least he was awake.

"You're inside a bullet. Think about something nice. Think about how hard I'm gonna fuck you later." Whip shifted, trying to easy the sudden tightness in his groin. Just the words made him wish it was *later* already.

Mitchell opened his mouth and laughed. "You are?" He kept his eyes closed, but a small smile played around his lips. "I hate this."

"You're afraid of speed?" Whip was one of the few Earth people who didn't share that particular affliction. Why was he so surprised that Mitchell did seem to be affected?

"When I was a kid, my one trip to Coney Island, I was the one sitting out the rides, holding everybody else's ice creams and balloons." Mitchell paled, even the memory clearly affecting him.

Boy, the apple had fallen far from the tree. Friday Otis Doombringer was the most fearless person Whip knew. He wondered what the hell had happened to Friday... He wasn't sure about Mitchell but suspected that something had caused his fear of so many things. Life must have assaulted him.

"Are you sure the stink gets better?" Mitchell gasped, turning slightly green. "It smells like three pigs farting in here."

"I ate lunch. So sue me." Their captain seethed at them. His teeth glinted menacingly in the half light.

Whip and Mitchell didn't say another word until they came to a dead stop in San Francisco. Whip pulled Mitchell out of the bullet's casing onto the train tracks.

"Is anyone waiting for us?" he asked the captain, turning around. The bullet, however, had already moved back a little and now reversed with blinding speed.

"Guess not." Whip took Mitchell's hand. "You okay?"

"Where are we?" Mitchell glanced around, but there were very few clues.

Whip took out his cell phone with his free hand checking his location, but he already suspected where they were. They climbed a set of stairs, ordinary street smells a certain comfort after the bullet train. "Civic Centre, Union Square, right under the BART station."

He pushed at a fire door. It wouldn't budge.

"Let me try." Mitchell dropped Whip's hand and shouldered the door. It blew off its hinges, landing on the street outside with a bang. Whip grinned as waves of dust and dirt flew around them. Maybe the apple hadn't fallen so far from the tree after all...

Mitchell took Whip's hand again and they rushed out into the noise and...they stopped.

"What the...?" Mitchell's head tried to go in ten directions in rapid succession.

A herd of water buffalo passed them. Water buffalo! On the streets of San Francisco! The animals moved around the fallen door, not missing a step. A group of orange-robed monks followed the parade of beasts as drummers in colourful outfits danced beside them, keeping time with huge drumsticks. Dancers in silks of rainbow hues accompanied the strange procession.

"It's the Lao New Year Festival!" Mitchell looked ecstatic.

Whip wasn't so thrilled. With all this chaos, he had to keep his wits about him, which was going to be hard with all this commotion around them. He had to look for their next guide...and also stay aware of danger. He had a feeling that whoever had tried to kill Mitchell wasn't about to give up. He couldn't be sure, but they felt very close.

Mitchell began to sway to the music, waving at a group of small children passing them in gaudy dragon masks. The children waved back. Whip felt churlish not joining in the fun. He lifted his hand, hoping for some sort of response or hint from their next guide, and as soon as he did, two trolls appeared on the other side of the procession staring at him and Mitchell.

Purs.

"Who are they?" Mitchell tensed beside him, staring at the fierce, ugly little men.

"They're purs. Very nasty trolls. They are not generally known to be helpful to humans. I've tangled with them a time or two. Their bite really fucking hurts. I suggest we keep moving." Whip pulled Mitchell beside him, surprised when a monk stepped out of the parade, stood in front of them and bowed.

"Friend or foe?" Mitchell asked Whip.

"Not sure. But I don't sense danger, even though he's smiling a lot. I say we go with the flow." Whip shrugged. They might as well see what happened.

The monk was tall and slim, his head shaved, and huge eyeglasses illuminating the longest lashes Whip had ever seen. The monk beckoned Whip and Mitchell.

"I really want to check in with my sister." Mitchell released Whip's hand, taking out his cell phone before Whip could stop him.

Alicia apparently didn't pick up as Mitchell left her a message while they followed the monk down a tiny street off Union Square. He led them to what looked like a soup kitchen.

This was definitely an unusual place for a superpowers meeting but stranger things had happened in Whip's life. The place was packed but smelt pleasantly of soup and chicken, the line of people waiting for food moving along at a brisk pace. The monk put his hands to Whip and Mitchell's backs, pressing them towards the line. A family of five lined up beside them.

"He thinks we're homeless," Whip whispered, absolutely appalled. Had the monk not been the expected guide after all? Maybe he was losing it…

"We're covered in soot and smoke and our backpacks leave a lot to be desired," Mitchell responded. "Maybe we shouldn't be surprised."

Whip glanced down to see two children staring up at him, mouths agape.

"Oh, great," he muttered in Mitchell's ear. "It's gonna be all over the news that Whip Jackson eats in soup kitchens."

"That's a great marketing gimmick," Mitchell said. He seemed to adapt to all of this with such...*élan*...that it was frightening. He took a tray off the pile and slid it across the bench in front of him. "Whip, pass this to the nice lady at the end of the row."

Whip pushed the tray down to the astonished woman who gave him a tentative smile. Mitchell cheerfully continued to slide trays down the line via Whip. "You want turkey with all the trimmings?" Mitchell asked him, looking feverish. They hadn't eaten so long ago, but bullet trains did weird things to one's equilibrium. Whip recalled how hungry he'd got the first time he'd ridden one, so he indulged Mitchell's apparent wild appetite.

They took their trays to a table behind them. The entire place had stopped. People were staring at them.

Oh, God...I hope my mom doesn't hear about this...

Whip kept a smile on his face as he sat beside Mitchell at a communal table.

"You should hand out some money," Mitchell said, keeping his voice low as he tucked into a plump slice of turkey.

"What do you mean?" Whip instantly regretted the question. He should have pretended he hadn't heard.

"*Get your wallet out and peel off some bucks.*" Mitchell's voice was now inside Whip's head. That was scary. He and Mitchell stared at one another for a moment. How was this possible? Disbelief seemed to have gripped Mitchell, too, because he muttered, "Somebody's recording you on their cell phone."

Oh, great. A homeless person with a camera phone. Mitchell must have heard his thoughts because he grinned, forking a pea into his mouth. He kept staring at Whip who shook his backpack from his shoulders and opened his wallet. He passed out several ones and fives. People fell over themselves trying to get to him.

"Give the twenty to the family we stood in line with," Mitchell whispered. It was amazing Whip could even hear him over the stampede.

"Not my *twenty.*" Whip was a generous man but growing up poor had left its mark. He hated not to have a single note in his wallet.

Mitchell's expression spurred him to action. He took the note and held it out to the mother now sitting beside him. She grabbed it and burst into tears. A few seconds later, after holding the note up to the light to check for a watermark, she threw her arms around him. Then he could smell it.

Purs.

They were somewhere close.

He sensed Mitchell's growing unease and, after a bit of a struggle, lifted his face from the mother's small, hard bosom. Wow, a homeless woman with a boob job. People in California sure didn't have their priorities straight.

"Thank you," she trilled. "Simone wants a Nintendo DS game for her birthday. I've had one on lay-away. This'll just about cover it!"

A homeless kid with a DS. Okay...

Mitchell's gaze was riveted to the two purs who must have followed them. Whip nudged Mitchell.

They stood as one. The purs were getting restless and attracting attention. Only their massive, bulbous noses were visible beneath their ski masks, protruding out of the middle of them.

"Sorry, gotta go," Whip announced, giving everyone a friendly wave.

"Bye!" the others shouted, six people reaching for Mitchell and Whip's trays before they'd even left the table. The purs came and stood in front of them.

"This way," one of them said, releasing a monsoonish gust of foul breath. These trolls were the kind typified by Hollywood movies.

Whip and Mitchell followed them outside, Whip desperate to lose them. He didn't trust these two creatures at all and planned to say something to Mr. Damek, the Earth House attorney from the esteemed firm of Arden, Bainbridge, Chinook and Damek. Damek was a nice guy, but the Native American attorney of the Lakota nations had a strange set of ethics. He felt all creatures, hideous and otherwise, deserved to be treated with respect. Fair enough. But he'd seen the otherwise elegant, handsome Damek sporting bandages across his face and hands after tangling with purs and Whip's least favourite variety of trolls, the mountain-dwelling risi. The risi were particularly unfriendly but that twit Goyathlay Damek seemed to delight in having them around his office.

"Risi," Whip said aloud as they rounded a corner. A small collection of trolls surrounded the tall, handsome, middle-aged Native American man in a smart, three-button suit, his long hair brushed out and gleaming.

As bright and shiny as Damek was, the risi, whose natural habitat was funeral mounds, looked especially grubby. It always surprised Whip since the risi were known to be the courtly, supposedly heroic trolls. In Whip's experience, they bit first then asked questions later.

Mr. Damek greeted him, with the tallest of the risi turning to glance at Whip.

"Mudshark," the risi said, his voice flat.

"Njáll." There was no love lost between them. Whip sensed immediately that nothing had changed. "Is this still about the lemonade incident?"

"Yes," Njáll said.

"Whatever," Whip responded. He put himself slightly in front of Mitchell in case Njáll got it into his pea-sized brain to bite the man. "Mr. Damek, this is—"

"I know who he is." Damek reached over the trolls' heads and shook Mitchell's hand. "Your uncle and I are great friends. I am pleased to learn he is alive and well. I've missed him. The entire Earth Court has missed him."

"How did you find out he's still alive?" Whip asked.

Damek glanced down and Whip noticed the troll who'd come to the hotel room to take him and Mitchell to the bullet train.

"You will have an armed escort until further notice," Mr. Damek said. "I expect you and Njáll to conduct yourselves as gentlemen."

Njáll grimaced at Whip, revealing two rows of jagged, sharp teeth.

Mitchell gasped at the sight of them.

Njáll swung him a look that could have stripped paint from a door.

"No problem," Whip said quickly, stepping back to put his hand at the small of Mitchell's back. "Where is the meeting?"

"At the bakery. Upstairs. Easter Sunrise has some special concoctions for you." Mr. Damek held a stone tablet in his hand. The man eschewed any modern conveniences, preferring all kinds of earth-based materials for his work, yet he was the most prepared and well-informed attorney Whip had ever met.

"I've given Njáll permission to take you the fast way," Mr. Damek said. "I'll be in touch, Whip. Mitchell, it's nice to meet you, and Njáll, stay away from lemonade, huh?"

Damek vanished before Njáll could sink his teeth into his arm.

"Grrr!" Njáll's arms flailed wildly as he regained his balance.

Mitchell looked pale. What a show-off the risi was.

"The bakery?" Whip asked, frankly afraid of being bitten himself. Njáll bared his teeth once more, raised his hands, waving his fingers until sparks shot from them, and they were off, reappearing right in front of Fabulous Cupcakes.

They brushed past the perennial line out front, several people squawking about the queue-jumpers. None of them could see the risi accompanying Whip and Mitchell, but Njáll suddenly turned to him.

"I want a cupcake."

The humans lined up for purchases looked down, searching for the source of the voice, puzzled expressions on their faces. Whip hoped the risi wasn't going to cause an incident.

"I'll get you one." Whip kept his arm around Mitchell's hips, urging him to the counter. Daine Paradis looked harried but broke into a smile when he saw them.

"Is that Njáll?" he asked, looking over the counter.

"It's me." Njáll rocked on his toes, looking flushed with happiness that Daine was acknowledging him.

"Your Majesty," Daine said, "I have two wonderful new flavours for you to try. How about a Guinness cupcake with Baileys Irish Cream frosting?"

"Sounds mighty good," Njáll squeaked.

"Who are you talking to?" a man at the counter asked.

"Me, you cretin." Njáll looked up, a dangerous expression in his eyes.

Daine slid the man a huge box. "Sorry for the wait, Stan. You can pay Annie over at the cash register."

"Okay. Thanks." Stan looked down, still unable to see the risi whose anger was rising fast.

"I also have a pink lemonade flavour with ginger lime frosting." Daine held up two cupcakes. "I'll put them on a tray. What would you like?" His glance went to Mitchell then shifted to Whip.

"One of each, thanks," Mitchell said.

"Me too," Whip echoed, hoping that Njáll wouldn't get snockered on the lemonade cupcake.

Daine loaded up a tray and nodded to Whip. "Take them upstairs. The huckleberry-raspberry and marshmallow ones are for my hubby. He's waiting for you."

Whip took the tray, following Njáll up the stairs.

"What was the lemonade incident?" Mitchell whispered to him.

"You'll see." Whip couldn't help but worry. As they reached the upstairs kitchen, Daine's cousin, Easter Sunrise, greeted them, a warm blast of baking cakes pleasantly wafting over them.

"Lemonade!" Njáll squeaked.

Too late to stop him, Whip watched the little troll's pudgy hands wrap around a glass. Ten seconds after swallowing a few gulps, he raced over to Easter, rubbing against her like a dog would hump a leg.

Whip noticed the astonished look on Mitchell's face.

Easter pushed the little risi into a chair. "Behave," she said.

"I can't. One whiff of lemonade and I'm the horniest bastard in the world."

"Here. Have this." She slid him a tiny blue cupcake.

"What is it?" Njáll sniffed it suspiciously.

"Blueberry."

"I'd rather have sexual relations with you," Njáll said.

"Excuse me." Whip reached a hand out to the risi's shoulder, squeezed, and the troll toppled from the chair and onto the floor.

"How long will he be out?" Easter asked.

"About ten minutes."

"I'd get going if I were you. He'll be so pissed when he wakes up." Easter rarely looked so worried, usually exuding calm and happiness.

"Yeah. I know." At least it gave them time to enjoy their cupcakes.

And enjoy them they did. Whip had a hard time refraining from eating Phillip's as well. But Daine would never forgive him if he did.

"Where is Phillip anyway? Wasn't he supposed to be here?" Whip wiped at the icing that was stuck to the corners of his mouth. No use wasting it, and he didn't have a strange reaction to lemonade so nothing stopped him from enjoying even one crumb.

Mitchell grinned at him as he frantically collected his own set of crumbs and made sure they all made it into his mouth.

"Phillip had to run ahead," Easter said, picking up a bowl of purple icing and giving it a vigorous stroke.

"Leave the cupcakes with me. I'll make sure they find a good home."

"Just as long as you let Daine know it wasn't my fault his husband didn't get them." Whip reached for Mitchell's hand, waiting for Easter to nod before pulling Mitchell towards the exit. "Let's go to your place. I want to see your uncle."

* * * *

Mitchell's family home turned out to be a gorgeous Victorian terrace on Baker Street in the heart of the tiny NoPa neighbourhood of San Francisco. NoPa — short for North of Panhandle — was a very hot, but tiny area known for its great restaurants and amazing Edwardian and Victorian houses.

The Dykins house was a typical terrace. Narrow, tall, and as soon as Mitchell unlocked the door, Whip could tell it was long. He was surprised how light, airy, and spacious it felt. Blond softwood floors shone throughout the place, the antique marble fire places, arched nooks, and high ceilings with their crown moulding and medallions giving a rich feel to the pale fawn-coloured walls with white trim.

Unadorned windows revealed views of the city skyline with the bay in the distance. A further glance showed that each window, including the magnificent bay windows in the living room, had shutters that receded into the walls. The house was a work of art.

Whip could see through the rooms all the way to the backyard that seemed to have several terraces. Mitchell seemed to hesitate.

"Mitchypoo?" Whip grinned when he caught the pained expression on Mitchell's face and followed Mitchell inside once he'd started moving again.

A young woman in a wheelchair zipped across three rooms to them, her arms outstretched to Mitchell. He rushed straight to her, hugging her. This had to be Alicia. Her eyes sparkled as she looked around her brother to Whip.

"Who's this handsome devil?" Alicia grinned.

"Whip Jackson," Mitchell said, introducing them.

"You're handsome. You single?" She was batting her eyelids at him.

Whip glanced at Mitchell.

"Aw…shoot. You play for his team, don't you?" She jerked her thumb towards her brother, her words more a statement than a question.

"Yes, ma'am." He was impressed how she could make him behave so easily.

"I've never been turned down so politely," she said. "I still think you're sexy. Turn around. Let me see your tushy."

He turned around.

"Very nice. Bet I could bounce quarters off 'em."

"Thanks."

They grinned at one another.

"Where's Foti?" Mitchell blurted.

"Who's Foti?" Whip asked, looking around for a dog.

"Our uncle." Mitchell kept his gaze on his sister, who shrugged.

Foti was what they called Friday Otis Doombringer? Whip couldn't have come up with that one if he'd tried.

Alicia seemed to be in a grumpy mood. "I have no idea. He was here, I made him lunch." She paused, giving her brother a hard look. "And he complained about it as usual. Next thing I knew the phone rang, he took the call then ran out of here."

Whip looked at Mitchell. "I thought you said he's blind and deaf?"

"He is. He sees shadows, though," Alicia said, "and he has a special phone that converts everything to Braille."

"That's handy," Whip said.

"He's into gadgets." Alicia looked bored. "Are you staying for dinner?" she asked Mitchell. "I'm sick of cooking just for me and that grumpy old man."

"It was only one night," Mitchell pointed out, but he seemed suddenly subdued.

The front doorbell rang and Mitchell opened it to Phillip Sedgwick and a slightly dazed-looking Njáll.

Mitchell explained that Foti had taken a call then disappeared.

"Any chance we can look at his phone?" Phillip asked Mitchell.

Alicia looked like she was about to argue, but Mitchell stepped in with a quick, "Sure."

He led the small procession to the telephone nook.

It was obvious that Alicia could see Njáll. "You're handsome," she said. "You single?"

Whip rolled his eyes as Phillip studied the phone. "How do we convert the Braille back to voice response?" he asked Mitchell.

Mitchell fiddled with some buttons.

"Neee-all," Alicia called out to the risi in a sing-song voice. Njáll seemed entranced by her as well. Oh, boy, she had to be hard up to have the hots for a demented troll.

Njáll giggled as she squeezed his butt cheeks. Whip was surprised he didn't tear her limb from limb.

"What did Easter give him?" Mitchell asked Phillip. "He's so...sweet all of a sudden."

"Blueberry icing. She's given me six tubs of it."

Mitchell fiddled with the buttons on Foti's phone some more. A man's voice suddenly came out of it, sounding agitated.

"Friday," the voice said, "I have bad news."

"What?" came the response.

"They know you're alive. I can't keep you safe anymore. I need to put you back into the Witness Trollection Programme."

"What's that?" Mitchell asked, but Whip spoke over him.

"That's Damek's voice!" Whip was stunned. "What the hell is going on?"

"Hey!" Njáll looked pissed as he shoved his way between Whip and Mitchell. "How can they put him in the WTP without my approval...or my authority?"

Oh, boy. Whip hoped that six tubs of blueberry icing would help keep the risi from exploding.

"I have no idea." Phillip looked furious as he pulled out his cell phone and called the attorney. They exchanged a few tense words.

"He wants us to stay here. I guess things are moving fast. He's picking up Justice Lashdown and says he'll be here in half an hour."

"Who is Justice Lashdown?" Mitchell asked.

"We'll get into that a little later." Phillip eyed Mitchell and Whip. "You two might want to get cleaned up. You're covered in dirt...or is it" — he leant forwards and sniffed, wrinkling his nose in disdain, or possible horror — "dung?"

Njáll went berserk. "You wanted 'em here fast and you got 'em fast and you know what they say, Mr. Sedgwick — shit happens!"

Phillip's eyes widened slightly. He stared down at the agitated risi. The little creature was so upset even the hairs in his massive ears became visible when he removed his balaclava. They actually twitched.

"Er…" Phillip reached into his jacket pocket and removed a small plastic container. He removed the lid and handed it to Njáll.

"Here, Commander Jørgensen, try some of this."

Njáll snatched the tub, inserting a long jagged fingernail into it, scooping the blue icing into his mouth, a blissful expression instantly crossing his hideous features.

"Come on," Mitchell said to Whip. "I'll show you to the guest room."

Whip followed Mitchell upstairs. The man seemed glum as he led Whip to a bright, spacious room with a four-poster bed and a magnificent view of the city from its gleaming windows.

"You okay?" Whip asked, dropping his backpack to the floor.

Mitchell nodded, but Whip knew he was in bad shape. "I know this is a lot to take in," he said. Mitchell nodded. Whip stepped forwards, removed the backpack from Mitchell's shoulders, dropped it beside his own and put his hands on Mitchell's face.

"It's okay. I know how disorienting it is and I didn't have a missing family member or a controversial death to deal with." He had no idea how Mitchell had managed to keep it together. There was a lot more to him than his somewhat conservative appearance had seemed to indicate. A *lot* more!

Mitchell's gaze flickered up to meet his. Whip could see the shock and confusion in his eyes. "What do you mean…controversial death? Who died?"

Whip mentally bitch-slapped himself. "I would rather you heard it from somebody else. I wasn't there. I'm assuming you're about to be told the truth..." Whip paused. "All I have is rumours. I was pleased to hear from you that he's alive and well." He put his hands to Mitchell's tense shoulders and squeezed. "We need a shower. Where is it?"

He felt the stress fall away from Mitchell and kept kneading. Mitchell moaned. "You have your own bathroom. Right here."

Whip reached around Mitchell and closed the door. "Come on. I want to be naked with you." He leaned in and kissed Mitchell, whose kisses came back hard and fast. They ripped off one another's clothes, their cocks springing to attention at one another.

"You do smell," Whip said, bending to kiss Mitchell's creamy shoulder.

"Back at you."

They grinned at each other. In the bathroom, Mitchell ran the shower faucets until the water turned steamy. They stepped into the hot spray, soaping each other. Whip longed to frolic with Mitchell again. He contented himself with stroking Mitchell's sweet cock. Their raging cocks made it hard to get too close to one another, but there was no time to indulge their passions. Both men stroked one another until Whip took a step back and turned on the cold water spray.

Whip gasped. "Tell me we're sharing a bed again tonight," he murmured.

"I hope so." Mitchell knelt before Whip and wound his arms around his knees. Damn. "Stroke yourself off for me," Mitchell commanded, "into my mouth."

Whip reached around to raise the temperature of the water again. He couldn't help it. The seductive sight of his cock filling Mitchell's mouth was more than he could take. He tugged at his cock, stroking it back and forth, his hand meeting the succulent, hot lips working to bring him pleasure.

Mitchell's hands kneaded Whip's ass, keeping his hips exactly where he wanted them. Whip felt the orgasm building, Mitchell taking over, Whip's hands falling away to pull back his dripping hair. Water beat down on Whip's head and shoulders as he came, blessed relief at last.

"Gotta suck your cock," he said to Mitchell.

Mitchell pulled off Whip, swallowing hard and topping off a killer blow job with a lingering kiss on Whip's cock.

"Oh, no. People are downstairs. I demand a rain check, though."

"It will be my pleasure." Whip turned off the taps. They grabbed a couple of towels, drying off fast. Whip felt fantastic. He couldn't stop grinning

"I'm going to my room to change." Mitchell wrapped a towel around his waist and leaned in for a quick kiss.

"Don't be long."

"I'll try not to be." Mitchell grinned at him and left Whip alone.

Whip ran some deodorant under his arms and rummaged through his backpack. The high-speed bullet train had penetrated the bag's fabric and left its stench on his clean garments. He found the least smelly pants and shirt he could find and threw them on.

"Ready?" Mitchell asked, poking his head round the door. He looked damned hot in his tight shirt and jeans with the button-down fly.

"Wow, you look hot."

"I do?" Mitchell looked surprised, glancing down at his outfit. "Thanks."

They headed downstairs together, Whip one step behind, his gaze on Mitchell's ass. *Damn*. He was starting to really like this guy. He rarely let any man into his bed more than a couple of times, but he was starting to dig Mitchell Dykins. He frowned to himself. It was a total fluke that the guy had beat him in the mudpit. This whole thing was a terrible nightmare that would soon go away.

He hoped.

Downstairs, a small group had assembled and stopped talking as soon as Mitchell and Whip walked into the room.

Whip took in the sight of Phillip and his partner Daine Paradis, Goyathlay Damek, Njáll and a couple of other trolls, and the Earth Court judge, Early Lashdown. Of all the elemental superpowers' court justices, Lashdown intrigued Whip the most. He was a down-to-earth guy...in more ways than one. He looked and dressed like a farmer but was hotter than hell and had superpowers that exceeded those of most other jurists in their realm. He could have been a movie star had he chosen that destiny, but instead had cultivated a civilian career as a cattle rancher.

What he really did was control natural disasters once they occurred. In his spare time he adjudicated superpower court cases. As he came across the room, extending his hand to Whip, the wrestler noticed that Early Lashdown wore jeans and cowboy boots really well.

"Whip," Judge Lashdown said, "sorry to hear you lost the fight with Mudpit Madman." He pointed towards Mitchell. "Everyone I know wants to see a rematch." He grinned as he shook Mitchell's hand. Whip detected a frisson of attraction spark between Mitchell and Judge Lashdown. Mitchell, however, stood close to him. Maybe he'd imagined the attraction.

"We were just discussing whether I had a right to be here," Phillip Sedgwick said as Njáll bounced impatiently beside him. "I've tried to explain to Njáll—Commander Jørgensen—that I am here in an unofficial capacity...as a friend. If you would like me to leave, I will. Daine and I both—"

"No," Mitchell said firmly. "I want you both to stay."

"So do I," Whip said.

"Where is my sister?"

"Resting comfortably in her room. She is taking a nap. She will awaken refreshed," Daine assured him. "I've left some green tea and raspberry cupcakes for her. She'll enjoy them when she wakes up."

"Thank you." Mitchell's concern for his sister was palpable. "That's so kind of you. You do so much for Alicia...for everyone."

"You're such a great guy, Daine," Whip said. Daine Paradis really was something of a local saint. He'd truly come into his own with Fabulous Cupcakes. Love and superpowers suited him. The man blushed. Despite his talents, he had no ego about his vocation.

Daine shuffled from one foot to the other. "Thank you. I'm glad to be of service."

Phillip kept a protective arm around his life partner, beaming at the praise heaped on Daine.

"Shall we sit down?" Mitchell asked. "Anyone want a drink?"

Early Lashdown shook his head. "No time for that. Here's the story in its most succinct form. Until this afternoon, nobody in the Earth House had any clue what had happened to your uncle. Friday simply vanished but under unusual circumstances." He paused. "He never said anything to you about the Mongolian death worm?"

Chapter Six

"The what?" Mitchell's jaw dropped. He glanced at Whip, hoping his new friend could help. But Whip looked as surprised as Mitchell felt. He turned back to the judge. "No. He never said anything. I would remember!"

"Do you recall anything unusual that happened on the third of March two years ago?" The judge didn't look away from Mitchell for even a second.

Mitchell lapsed into silence, thinking hard. "Specifically...no. Not really." He lifted his shoulders feeling inadequate. "What I remember is that my sister was having some severe health issues at that time. She'd developed bowel and bladder problems as a result of the wheelchair she'd been using." His voice trembled. The memory was horrible.

"I almost lost her." He kept his gaze on an imaginary spot in the middle distance. It was an old meditation technique that helped calm him. "I'd been in touch with Foti, my uncle, on and off over the years. He is my mother's brother and Alicia and I are fond of him. I was struggling to hold onto this house because

I'd lost my job." He dropped his voice. "And taking care of Alicia's medical expenses wasn't easy. Not everything was covered by insurance. Foti's phone call around that time—"

"When?" the judge pounced on him.

Mitchell had to think. "At some point in February. He suggested he could move in and help pay the mortgage. It just seemed...perfect. He started spending a lot of time here. At first, I must admit, it was a huge relief having help for my sister. I didn't want to ask him for rent. Then..."

He became silent, struggling with the emotions the memory caused. It was hard to sort through all of them to get at the facts. "He disappeared for a few days. I remember that."

"And what happened?" Judge Lashdown's tone was coaxing.

"I hate talking about him. Foti is so private. He disappeared...like I said. Alicia and I got worried then he suddenly turned back up one night. He could hardly see and he couldn't hear at all, but he came home." Mitchell stopped speaking, a little overwhelmed. Nobody said anything. Everyone seemed riveted. "I realise now I shouldn't have listened to him. I should have taken him to a doctor, but he had this strange man with him who said we had to look after him."

Mitchell lapsed into an anxious silence. "Of course...I took care of him. At first it was awful. He was helpless. Especially when he became completely blind. It was hard. I mean taking care of my sister was a commitment and then I had Foti. But... I know it sounds weird, but he seemed to thrive. He stopped being afraid after the first few weeks. He still hardly leaves the house and he's marvellous with Alicia. He really loves her and sometimes I forget he is blind and deaf. He sort of...takes care of us both now."

Judge Lashdown smiled. "That's what I hear. His caseworker said he fooled you both."

"Fooled us?" Mitchell was stunned.

"Well...I won't say he's in full possession of his faculties, but tamping them down, going into hiding here...helped keep him off the radar. Whoever went after him in the beginning when all this started obviously realises Friday is alive and that you have inherited his remarkable abilities," the judge said. "So, I'm afraid, an executive meeting is in order. We need to go."

"Go? Where are we going?" Mitchell's throat was suddenly dry.

"Where else?" the judge said in a tone that suggested that Mitchell was incredibly stupid. "The Temple of Poi."

* * * *

In all the years Mitchell had lived in San Francisco he had never been to the famous Temple of Poi. His sister and Foti went regularly. It had become their 'thing' and he had never intruded on their shared passion. All he knew was that the SOMA, or South of Market Street district, establishment taught dance.

Alicia loved it because she took fan and poi ball classes. These strengthened her arms and allowed her a measure of independence. She could wheel herself up and down some of the scariest streets in San Francisco now, thanks to the workouts she got.

Foti just loved the place. Mitchell looked around as they approached it. Whip stood beside him as they checked out the big windows. He could tell that the building was packed. Tiki torches shone outside, lights blazed inside.

Mitchell was surprised to see various heavily populated classes taking place. A different type of music played for each, and the hands and feet of the participants moved in a variety of ways. One class to his left seemed to be a martial arts style lesson with students wielding wooden staffs. To his right, a poi dance class was being held with Polynesian music wafting from the room. Poi balls — small white balls dangling from threads — swung rhythmically in the air as dancers swayed to the music. Some of the students had weights on the ends of their cords. The spinning effect of the dancers' performance was quite…hypnotic.

"It's run by a fabulous woman called Glitter Girl and she teaches staff, poi, fan, and hoop dancing," Whip told him. "These are basic Fire arts, but fire isn't necessary to do these classes. They are designed to help people understand themselves, to give them balance and poise through movement."

"But why are we here?" Mitchell was so confused.

Whip looked like he knew more but bit his lip and seemed to be waiting for somebody else to speak.

"It's a great cover," Mr. Damek said. "Glitter Girl lets anyone who needs spiritual asylum use the basement." He paused. "And right now, we have a need."

He led the small procession around the back of the building where two trolls stood guard outside what looked like a cellar door. It creaked open, a dank smell emerging from it.

Mitchell peered inside. He blinked. All he could see and smell was dank darkness. "Somebody needs to turn on a light," he said.

"What's going on?" Whip asked, right beside him. Mitchell heard a scuffle and Whip was gone.

"I'm sorry," Mr. Damek said, suddenly appearing beside Mitchell. "I was afraid you'd say no. Your uncle has shirked his responsibilities long enough. If he can't perform, the next male family member in line must step in. It's in his contract."

"It's a mudpit," Mitchell said, realising too late that nobody had moved, except for Whip who was screaming out to him to run. His voice sounded slightly hollow, coming out of the darkness that was apparently hiding another one of those horrendous mudpits.

"I know." Mr. Damek gave him a shove that sent Mitchell flying right into the filthy slush.

Mitchell gasped, his mouth immediately filling with dirt and sand. *Damn*, he hated mud. He spat the filth out as best he could but the sudden feeling of losing ground made him realise there was a bigger danger. He started sinking, his arms and legs flailing in a gesture that was as instinctual as it was useless.

"You must fulfil your destiny!" Damek's voice rang in his ears, the sound echoing around him.

Mitchell felt an earthquake coming. He'd never been so pissed in his life. Damek's voice drifted away, replaced by what seemed like thousands of voices screaming, "Madman! Madman!"

He free-fell for several seconds, sucked from the mud back into air, his voice hoarse from his own screaming. He saw a wooden floor below him and tried to brace himself for the fall but he seemed to be in some sort of slippery well, his fingers and toes unable to grasp onto the walls' slimy surface. He tried to ball himself up but landed hard on a heavy door that appeared out of nowhere. The door creaked open, dropping him down…down…into a cool blue pool.

The audience's mantra filled his soul. They were calling for him…the mudpit wrestling version of him, that was.

"You took your time," a small man said to him. He was short but had matinee-idol good looks. He was blond, blue-eyed and…

Mitchell had never found himself attracted to dwarves but this one was hot.

"Who are you?" Mitchell asked as he swam around in the increasingly warm liquid, fully clothed, trying to keep his head above the surface.

"You've forgotten me already?" the dwarf asked, pacing the edge of what Mitchell now realised was a sumptuous Olympic-size swimming pool.

Steam rose from the water in pleasant, odourless drifts. He gazed out of the softly lit windows. All he could see was dirt and hard-packed stone. It was the same view he'd observed during his soul retrieval with Carrie Hoffman. Man, was she involved in all of this?

"Sir, I am Bixby, since you've forgotten. Now the mud has entered your pores, you can remove your clothes. Leave them here." He pointed to the tiled area beside him.

Mitchell scrambled to get out of his wet clothes and shoes, but Bixby shook his head when Mitchell tried to climb out of the pool.

"Stay in." Bixby seemed awfully mad about something.

A door opened, releasing a shard of brilliant light and a burst of voices chanting, "Madman! Madman!"

Naked, Mitchell kept moving around until Bixby cut into his anxious thoughts.

"You can get out now."

Mitchell swam to the side, walking up the stairs. Bixby met him with a fluffy white towel, his gaze level with Mitchell's crotch. The door slowly closed of its own accord. Two more dwarves, dressed completely in white, hurried over to him.

"Sauna," Bixby said over his shoulder. "He's worse off than I thought."

"Worse? What's that supposed to mean?" Mitchell asked as the dwarves grabbed his hands and took him to a small booth. The door opened. Mitchell could hardly breathe it was so hot inside. The dwarves pushed him on to the wooden bench, one of them sitting behind him. The other poured water onto the sauna's hot stones with a wooden ladle.

The temperature whoomped to almost unendurable heights. Mitchell glanced at a thermometer on the wall but the dwarf behind him turned his head away from it. He began massaging Mitchell's shoulders, talking rapidly. Mitchell didn't know what to do but surrender to the pleasure of the release of the tension in his shoulders. He closed his eyes, ripples of pain flowing down his neck and arms.

"You're so tight," the dwarf complained. "Ya gotta relax, Madman."

"Mitchell." Getting his name out was tough. It was hard to do anything but moan now that the other dwarf was kneading his feet and calves. He was worried about getting an erection. It felt so good. Something warm spread over his arms. Oil.

"Gotta slick you up, Madman," the dwarf said, ignoring Mitchell's directive to call him by his given name.

Suddenly, Mitchell found himself being yanked to his feet, his two attendants rushing him out of the sauna. The drop in temperature shocked him, as did the flurry of hands oiling up his body. Somebody slid skin-tight red trunks up his thighs. He felt somebody cupping his balls and stroking his cock.

He looked down and gaped. "Bixby! What the—?" He tried to step back but too many hands kept working on his muscles, oiling his body.

Bixby looked indignant. "I'm your fluffer," he said. "Gotta get you frisky before your fight."

"Fight? I don't want to fight." Mitchell felt uncomfortable with all of this, especially the way Bixby was manhandling him.

"You'd better wanna fight. You could die in the ring otherwise." The trunks reached Mitchell's hips. Tight, sexy trunks with a gun painted on the crotch. He could tell because he now stood looking at himself in a mirror. He didn't resemble himself, but yet he did. He looked like a larger-than-life version of himself with black leather motorcycle boots—where the hell had they come from?—and the red trunks that revealed...everything.

"See?" Bixby ran his hand across Mitchell's crotch. "Got you revved up enough to make your senses tingle...but not horned up enough to distract you. Now go get him!"

"Who?" Mitchell had no idea what the hell was going on.

"Mudshark Jackson, of course." Bixby shoved him into a dark passageway and the dwarves accompanied him...nay, they frogmarched him, towards the deafening sound of applause and cheering.

"The troll-tossing contest's almost over," Bixby said, his voice coming out of the dark.

"I don't want to fight Mudshark. I *like* Mudshark." Mitchell had delightful mental images of frolicking naked with the man.

"Yeah? Well, he don't like you. He went to the court and demanded a rematch. He don't like gettin' beat."

"He did?" This was shocking news to Mitchell. Had it been Whip, Mudshark, or the strange man posing as Mudshark who'd gone to the court?

"I don't wanna fight him. Wait." Mitchell looked down, trying to see Bixby in the thick, stifling darkness. "Does Mudshark have a fluffer?"

"Of course he does. I hear they get it on all the way."

That did it. Mitchell lost his cool completely. He understood it was irrational to feel so jealous, but he couldn't help it.

The doors swung open and the crowd rose to its feet. The rumble beneath his motorcycle boots flew up his legs and infused his body with a barely controllable rage. He walked to the caged ring, a team of mud-covered trolls exiting the dirty arena as he got closer, all of them giving him friendly waves. The crowd chanted his name as Whip walked in from the diagonally opposite direction, his trademark white underpants with the grenade looking shinier than ever. He filled the pants well. Mitchell saw the hostile stare on Whip's face and swallowed. The crowd seemed to want blood. The two wrestlers stood outside the cage on opposite sides.

Whip's face showed a murderous fury that would have surprised Mitchell had he not realised this must be Mudshark. He looked so much like Whip, it was uncanny. How was Mitchell supposed to deal with his emotions? In many ways he was looking at a total stranger, all the man's humanity, kindness and…lust for Mitchell gone. On the other hand, he looked so much like Whip…

He hates me. He really hates me! The disappointment was impossible to ignore.

Mitchell was stunned when the crowd fell silent. Dancers of all kinds twirled and whirled into the arena, dancing with fiery poi balls, hula hoops set on fire and the *pièce de résistance*, hand fans that disappeared with puffs of heart-shaped smoke.

The music consisted of loud hypnotic taiko drums, wielded by some of the tallest women Mitchell had ever seen. He wondered if they were giants. He gazed at their short, golden tunics, lace-up sandals, their astonishing muscles and…

No, he realised.

Amazons.

He'd always thought they were a myth. The sound of the drums reverberated in his ears until the women stopped, leant back with golden bows, and shot arrows into the air. The arrows rose and fell, coming back to the mudpit, landing in a circle of fire in the middle of the ring. A sound of trumpets came from somewhere and a gorgeous, golden woman emerged in colours of the sunset, wielding four pairs of poi balls in each hand. She stood, triumphant, in the centre of the ring.

Alicia.

She was standing! Painted gold, her hair falling in long tresses from a tiara made of what looked like bark and tree leaves, his sister looked incredible. She threw up her arms and the poi balls all ignited. She gave Mitchell a quick wink as she began to entertain the crowd. As fast as she'd appeared, she took a bow and *poof*, disappeared. Overcome with emotion, he longed to touch her…to talk to her.

Alicia materialised beside him, her lips and eyes shimmering with gold dust.

"Surprised?" she asked, kissing his cheek.

"What…how?"

"Here, I am the queen," she said. "Good luck. Make me proud."

She vanished in a gust of gold glitter that rose and fell like little fireflies settling on the four corners of the ring. Across the arena, he glimpsed Whip—the *real* Whip—waving frantically at him. Mitchell watched two soldiers dressed like Greek warriors with short white tunics, marching him towards the other Whip Jackson. No. Towards the Mudshark version. God, this was confusing.

Whip still had on the shirt he'd been wearing when they first arrived, but was otherwise clad only in his white underpants. The shirt soon came off and he stood beside the other Whip.

What the hell was going on?

The Snake, the man Whip had previously beaten, appeared beside Mitchell, wearing the same red trunks Mitchell was. The cage doors creaked open of their own accord, the crowd demanding action. *Oh, no.* Mitchell had to take on both Whips…with the loony Emir 'The Snake' Putin standing in his corner.

Oh, hell, no. The Snake is a nut bar.

"You bettah fight good," The Snake sneered.

A hush fell over the crowd and to Mitchell's astonishment he heard the sound of a horse's hooves. The crowd began taking photos, applauding, whistling and shouting, "Go, Lavrentios! Go, Lavrentios! La-Vren-Teeeee-Os!"

The crowd kept up the chant as the most astonishing, gorgeous creature Mitchell had ever seen cantered into the arena then into the ring on a golden carpet that inexplicably appeared in front of him as he advanced. Mitchell had never seen anything like it.

A centaur.

His human half was total Greek god, his equine half a gleaming black stallion. He was lean, but muscular, his face elegant and sensual. His long, equine black hair gleamed under the bright, hot lights of the centre stage. He took the microphone from one of the dancers.

"Ladies and gentlemen," the centaur intoned in a heavy European accent. "It is said I was sired by an unholy union between a human and an Elemental Earth god, but what you are about to see is a match that defines the meaning of Hell!"

The crowd roared, people jumping to their feet, stomping, screaming, doing the wave.

It was frightening.

The centaur's voice drowned out even the astounding level of noise produced by a crowd whipped into a frenzy by their own expectations. "Hell in a cell! Ladies and gentlemen, I present to you the Mudsharks versus The Snake and Madman, our newest sensation."

More noise.

The centaur galloped towards Mitchell. "I present to you, Mitchell 'Madman' Dykins, nephew of one of our greatest warriors, Friday Otis."

As the crowd's collective screams rose to a deafening pitch, Mitchell felt a moment of panic. He gazed around the arena. The only people he recognised were the Whips and his own lunatic fighting partner. He gulped. He didn't want this fight. He hadn't wanted the last one either. He needed to find a way out, but he had no time to think about things. The opening bell rang as the centaur galloped out of the arena and the crowd went bonkers.

Both Whips lunged for him and The Snake. The Snake sneered at him.

Something ignited in Mitchell and he went for his pit partner, who looked surprised. One of the Whips took Mitchell down. He wasn't sure which version it was but he hated the laughter that accompanied the waist lock Whip gripped him in. Whip dragged Mitchell to his feet and began parading around the ring with Mitchell in a headlock. The crowd roared with laughter. Mitchell felt a white-hot rage flare behind his eyes as he pulled back and grabbed Whip with one arm, dragging him into the mud.

The fight was on. Both participants grappled for supremacy, writhing all over each other in the mud. It was so homoerotic, Mitchell couldn't believe it. Mitchell accidentally kicked The Snake in the back of the head and the behemoth flopped face down into the mud. Six trolls entered the ring and dragged The Snake out. Two paramedics tended him ringside as Mitchell fought the two Whips on his own. They were brutal and tough and he was surprised when he took down one of them with an elbow drop, getting the other into a full body lock of his own.

"Jesus Christ!" Whip roared in his ear as he squirmed and battled in a futile way underneath him. "I'm gonna fuckin' *kill* you!"

Mitchell laughed. He stood, Whip flailing in the mud. The fight was over. Whip lay staring up at Mitchell in disbelief. He got to his knees long after the count, with the assistance of two trolls who danced in victory around Mitchell.

"I couldn't move. It was like death sand," Whip screamed at the ref who held Mitchell's hand up in victory.

The crowd went crazy, but Mitchell wasn't happy. Whip detested him and the fight had brought out a part of himself he didn't particularly like—a hateful, hurtful part he associated with his mother. For a few moment there, he had revelled in the violence, had wanted to hurt Whip. He despised that. He shuffled off to his dressing room to clean up and change, surrounded by strangers who thought he was fantastic but really didn't give a shit about him.

"Aren't you happy?" Bixby asked as he shoved Mitchell towards the pool again.

"Hell, no. I want my life back. I want things to get back to normal."

"Normal? My dear boy, you've just walked into your power. You think you're gonna find normal again?"

"Yes. Why not?" Mitchell gasped when Bixby kicked him into the pool. The water was nice and warm and seemed to soothe his now aching body.

"Good luck with that, boy."

"Why do you keep calling me boy?" Mitchell asked. "You can't be much older than me."

"Guess again. I'm one hundred and seventy-two."

Before Mitchell could respond, he was sucked out of the pool, up the dark, horrible well, back into the mudpit, which was now dry. Frantically, he scrabbled around the hard-packed earth, naked except for his red fighting pants. He ran for the door where it had all started it all. With an effort that made his muscles scream in pain, he yanked it open and found himself falling out onto the street.

It was dark and quiet. The city seemed to be asleep.

And he was all alone. He shivered with cold as he began to run home, hoping this had all been a horrible nightmare. He didn't want to be Mudpit Madman. He didn't.

He just wanted to go home.

* * * *

Whip opened his eyes to bright daylight filtering through the gauzy curtains covering the window. The bed was still there, Mitchell lay next to him, his face relaxed in sleep and his mouth half open as he snored softly, the sheet pulled up to under his chin.

So far, so good.

He looked towards the nightstand to check the time. Had the alarm clock always looked like a cupcake? *Holy shit.* Not good. This was not the hotel room. There'd been a boring functional timepiece there—black and serious-looking. This one was…colourful to say the least. He was back in Mitchell's guest bedroom. As he tried to figure out what had happened, he realised his body ached as if he'd been in the ring all night. *Again*?

Had they fought each other? No…it must have been a dream.

When he lifted his head to look at himself, the eerie feeling of lying in mud proved to be correct. Shit, and his head was about to explode.

What the hell is going on?

Whip was *covered* in mud. He sat up, lifted the sheet away to check Mitchell and discovered that he was dirty, not really muddy. And he wore the damned red pants with the image of a revolver on them. Shock made him drop the sheet back.

Holy crap. I didn't *imagine it.* Last night Mitchell had taken him down the way his uncle used to sucker-punch his opponents, making the mud cooperate and imprison them. Friday had taught him how to beat it but he hadn't had to use the sleeping mud manoeuvre for…aeons. He hadn't even remembered it until just now. Except—it shouldn't have been possible for Mitchell to do that. Only one…

Holy mother-effing crap! He has Friday's power. He is king of the Earth.

Did Mitchell even realise it? He now had the ability to make the very foundation on which they stood shake, rattle, roll…and kill.

"What the fuck?" Mitchell suddenly sat up next to him and stared at all the mud. As the sheet slid farther down his body, revealing more dirt, it became obvious that the truth of the previous night's events was becoming clear to him too. Mitchell's eyes widened and he looked at Whip. "This is stupid…"

"I agree. It is getting ridiculous." Whip stretched his aching muscles and winced as his back popped. He'd been a fighter for a while, but these last few encounters had taken it out of him much more than normal. He almost chuckled. *That's because they weren't*—normal *encounters, that is.* Superpowers were apparently involved, and not the peaceful kind from the looks of it.

"I thought it was just a dream." Mitchell frowned and tried to stroke the dirt off his chest, only succeeding in smearing it all over the place. Some of the mud from Whip's body had transferred to Mitchell's body and didn't appear to want to leave him. This was obviously some kind of special mud, not just your normal house and garden variety.

"You remember what happened?" Whip looked up from his own ineffectual attempts to get clean.

"What? No, it was a dream." Mitchell tilted his head, his face ashen now. "Wasn't it?"

"I don't know." Whip shrugged. "As weird as this has been—and with you clearly immune against the personality split, or whatever it is—who knows?"

"I fought you and...*you*."

"You and The Snake. I appear to have an alter ego who is really someone else disguising himself as me. As far as I can tell, the fight promoters like the fact that this guy is posing as me. Two Whips in the ring. They forced me into the fight last night. I was so mad!"

"I'm sorry." Mitchell looked crestfallen.

"You didn't do anything. I saw the way they shoved you in head first." He paused, trying to assemble his thoughts. "You know what? This guy posing as me could very well be the killer we're looking for."

"You could be right." Mitchell rubbed his upper arms as if to warm himself. "Do you think it's connected to what happened to my uncle? You've never explained...this controversial death you mentioned. And from the looks of things, nobody else will tell me, either. What happened?"

"I need a shower. And coffee. Then I'll explain." Whip didn't look forward to it, but it had to be done. Maybe once Mitchell knew everything, they'd be able to figure out what to do about all the weirdness.

Mitchell looked dejected. "Okay." He studied a couple of broken fingernails. "The aches and pains...all of this would explain why my whole body hurts like hell. I've *really* been fighting you all night. Well, not you—it was actually Mudshark."

"Yeah, but *I'm* Mudshark. You beat the shit out of me." Whip didn't understand how that was even possible, and he swore they were going to get to the bottom of it. This couldn't go on. He didn't want to hurt like this all the time.

"I'm sorry, Whip." Mitchell was all over him, his expression stricken.

Whip pushed him back. "I'm in a lot of pain from the fight."

"I'm sorry." Mitchell looked dejected as he moved away.

"No. Stop saying that. It's not your fault." Whip swung his legs over the side of the bed, determined to stick to his course of action and not be distracted by Mitchell's amazing body. Already mostly undressed for him, no less. "The real problem is that if word from the underground hits the streets, my name will be...mud. Pardon the pun. What good am I as the leader of the World Wide Wrestlers team if a rank amateur beats me? Twice in a row?" He glanced over his shoulder at Mitchell. "No offence."

"None taken." Mitchell perked up as if that explanation made it better. "But I think it has gone too far. We need help."

"Probably." The thought had occurred to him, but whom could they ask? They had no idea who could be trusted and who was a traitor. He shuddered as another thought hit him. "Do you have any idea how you won the fight?"

"No, you said you couldn't move. But did I do that?" Mitchell frowned.

"Yes, you did."

"I don't get it. How can I do something like that without wanting it? Without even knowing *how*?"

Mitchell gave up on the cleaning efforts, shot Whip a bleak look and cast a longing look at the bathroom.

"I guess you don't get it, but neither do I. And you're right—it's time I told you what's been going on. At least the part that I *do* understand." Whip stood, held out a hand for Mitchell, pulling him up with him. "I may not like someone beating me, but I think I can deal with it. Mudshark, on the other hand, may have a problem with it."

"Shit." Mitchell paled and stopped walking. "You think he'll try to kill me again, don't you?"

"I think it's very possible." Whip didn't really want to deal with it right now. He needed to get clean, drink a gallon of coffee and work through the riddle. In that order.

They showered together, but even though Mitchell's body was especially tempting, all wet and slippery like that, Whip wasn't really in the mood for passion. There was too much going on in his head—too many questions were demanding answers.

They dried off and dressed, Mitchell lending Whip some clean clothes from his stash. Whip liked the package of new Calvin Klein boxer briefs Mitchell tossed to him. They cheered him up. The black pair he selected made him feel sexy. Wearing the man's shirt and jeans made him feel dirty-sexy. If he wasn't so depressed about the fight he'd jump Mitchell's bones, never mind the need for explanations.

Down in the kitchen, Mitchell made coffee as Alicia whizzed around in her wheelchair. She air-kissed them both claiming she had a class to attend. She left the house with a Paratransit driver after his assistant had helped her down the stairs.

"Did I imagine it or did she stand up in the ring last night?" Whip asked as soon as he heard the front door close.

Mitchell whirled around to him. "I was going to ask you the same thing! How about the centaur…?"

"I've seen him before. A mercurial asshole. And the Amazons. They're something, aren't they?" Whip grinned at the memory.

Mitchell poured them each a cup of coffee, doctored Whip's the way the man liked with a little milk and half a teaspoon of sugar, and they moved to the kitchen table. Whip was pleased they were alone. It would help not having Alicia—or anybody else— around. He had a feeling that wouldn't last.

Chapter Seven

"I feel guilty about my job," Mitchell said—a total non sequitur.

It derailed Whip a little. Hadn't he been about to explain things? What had made Mitchell mention his job all of a sudden? When Mitchell's house phone rang, Whip just rolled his eyes. Apparently, nothing was going to go as planned.

Mitchell got up and checked the readout on the kitchen bench top. He made a face. "It's Larry Parker. I should take it. Bet he's gonna bawl me out for doing practically nothing the last couple of days."

Mitchell's eyes widened after what must have been only the first few words. He put Larry on loudspeaker so Whip could hear.

Larry apparently loved the job Mitchell was doing. He adored the PR stunt of Whip dining in a soup kitchen. *PR stunt. Right.* Nevertheless, intentional or not, apparently it was all over the Internet.

"You're unorthodox, Dykins!" Larry boomed down the phone. "I was a little worried about hiring you. I thought you'd be a real stuffed shirt, but I'm glad you proved me wrong. And getting into the ring in that underground fight was a stroke of genius." He paused. "Genius! Listen, keep doing what you're doing. I can't believe they raised a hundred thousand dollars last night for crippled children. You're makin' me look good, dude. What other ideas you got on the boil?"

Mitchell looked dazed. "Nothing's locked in yet, but I'll keep you updated."

"Awesome. I expect to see you at our weekly brainstorming session at noon."

Whip and Mitchell eyed the wall clock. It was just after nine in the morning. Mitchell ended the call and returned to the table. "I can't believe it. He thinks I'm doing a great job."

"You are." Whip grinned at him. "For now. I think things are gonna get a little hairy so we need to be in sync. I'll keep the explanation brief, but I still think we need help." He took a deep breath. "You know by now that your uncle was a great wrestling champion. He had a gift, a unique ability to make mud imprison his opponents. I've never experienced anything like it, before or since...until last night."

Mitchell stared at him.

Whip sipped his coffee. "Look, he called the trick *sleeping mud* because it could render an opponent into a catatonic state within minutes. He had power over it and never used mud to maim—as he said, only to contain. The problem is that two years ago after teaching me and a couple of other...disciples...he cherished how to combat the mud, he had a fight and the opponent died. It was horrible. I will never forget his screams. When they pulled 'Malicious' Mick Kerrigan out of the mudpit, his head and shoulders were missing. Just gone."

"Oh, my God." Mitchell's sudden hand movement sent his coffee flying.

They scrambled to clean up the liquid from the table and floor, Whip continuing his story.

"It was a Mongolian death worm that killed him. It was hidden in the dirt. Some say they are a myth, but I saw that thing. I saw it balloon to several feet to kill Mick. Your uncle was horrified. He said he would never conjure up such a vicious creature to beat an opponent. He said the worm was planted in there. Many of us saw it, but then it vanished. I saw your uncle fight valiantly try to save Mick Kerrigan. He was devastated that day. He was supposed to go on trial. Some people said his attempt at saving Mick was a scam...all for show. Others believe he'd been set up by another wrestler who was jealous of him."

"And what do you believe?" Mitchell asked, kneeling on the floor, rag in hand.

"I believe your uncle. I suspect whoever the killer was must be powerful and that your uncle went into the Witness Trollection Programme to turn court's evidence against him. Then...you and I met. I guess we woke a sleeping dragon."

Mitchell grinned. "You woke up *my* sleeping dragon, honey."

They crawled across the floor to one another and began to kiss.

Mitchell's landline rang again.

"Don't answer it," Whip begged. They kissed until they heard the voice message coming in. It was Daine Paradis.

"I'm worried about you both. They wouldn't give me and Phillip access to the fight last night. It was awful. But listen, I'm proud of you and the money you raised for the children's charity. I've even developed a special mudpie cupcake in your honour. You both need to come and taste-test the recipes. I'm going to donate the first week's sales to the same charity so you have to get here right now!"

"Crap," Mitchell said. "Just when I thought I was about to get lucky."

"Let's go over, get some vittles and then get each other." Mitchell winked.

Whip felt better every second at the prospect.

They'd dumped their coffee cups in the sink and were about to leave when the front doorbell rang.

Whip, now operating in full protective mode, got to the door first, looked through the side window panels and grinned when he saw Daine and Phillip brandishing several plastic containers.

"You know what they say about mountains and Muhammad," Daine said, as soon as Whip had opened the door. "We thought we'd bring the party here."

Over more coffee, which Daine made and somehow seemed to turn into an aphrodisiac as far as Whip was concerned, they taste-tested tons of cakes in the kitchen. The events of the previous night unravelled.

"I think you're in danger," Phillip said, finally.

They'd all decided the mudpie with tin roof sundae topping was outstanding and by now, Whip was frantic with desire for Mitchell. They sat back in the kitchen chairs, observing the wreckage of cake crumbs and paper cups.

"I think the dark chocolate icing with gold dust was inspired." Mitchell licked his fingers, throwing a meaningful look in Whip's direction.

"You put something in that coffee." Phillip sighed. "I'm as horny as hell for you, Daine."

"Really." It was a statement. Not a question. Daine wriggled around on his chair, beaming at his lover.

"Use the spare room at the top of the stairs," Mitchell said, rising and grabbing Whip's hand.

"This conversation isn't over," Phillip called out after them.

But sense and sensibility had to wait. Whip wanted Mitchell so bad nothing else mattered.

In his room, he shut and locked the door. He didn't want to think about sleeping mud, Mongolian death worms or a killer impersonating him. He wanted the man now kissing him. He took hold of Mitchell in his arms, loving the taste of chocolate on his tongue.

"Time for the real dessert treat." Whip dragged his laughing lover back towards the bed.

It was getting awfully late — Mitchell had a meeting — and on top of the long hard night in the ring they'd had he should have been a lot more tired. Somehow, he just couldn't feel the exhaustion. It was probably Daine's coffee. No — it was Mitchell's tempting ass, and thinking of what he was going to do with it... That did it. Their clothes came off within seconds.

He fell onto his back, pulling Mitchell on top of him so the slender man wouldn't get hurt. What was he thinking? Mitchell was a frickin' powerhouse in the mudpit.

Twinkling blue eyes looked straight at him as Mitchell lowered his head, touching their lips for a brief kiss. God, the man's flavour was now enhanced by the mudpie they'd just eaten, and Whip slid up a hand to hold Mitchell's head steady as he explored the hot mouth with his tongue.

Mitchell moaned and melted against him, kissing back with a fervour that fired Whip's libido to unimagined heights. He really did want to eat the man up, and soon kissing wasn't enough. With a quick move made easy from many years in the ring, he turned them around so that Mitchell was underneath, blinking up at him with the most adorable look of confusion ever.

He focused on embracing that confusion away by placing little kisses all over the man's face. Starting with the forehead and eyes, he kissed and licked his way down one cheek, then back up the other. Mitchell pushed his groin upwards, grinding their erections together, as Whip continued his loving, oral assault down Mitchell's neck then along his collarbone. He made his way to a nipple and licked it into a pebbled little nub that was straining for more attention. The other one got the same treatment and Mitchell grabbed his hair to hold his head where he wanted it.

After giving both stiff nipples enough attention to make them all red and puffy, Whip slid down and licked a path to Mitchell's straining cock. He took it in hand to hold it steady and licked from base to tip.

"Shit." Mitchell's hips bucked. "So good."

Whip grinned. He loved how responsive Mitchell was and renewed his efforts to drive his lover absolutely insane with lust. Cock and balls were item one on his list, and from the sounds Mitchell was soon making, he was doing a good job. He sucked and licked everywhere he could reach before sliding down farther to spread Mitchell's unresisting legs enough to see his prize.

The tight little pucker was too tempting to resist, not that he tried. He licked a wet path from the top of Mitchell's crack, across the wrinkled skin and all the way past the perineum up along the ball sac to the tip of Mitchell's cock.

Mitchell wailed and his head started thrashing from left to right on his pillow when Whip repeated his slow perusal of the tempting skin a few more times. It was softer than any he'd ever encountered, and he loved that Mitchell was close to hairless down there. The few little hairs he encountered were a delicious change in feeling that he treasured as his tongue slid along them.

"Please!" Mitchell's voice was husky, his hands balled into fists where they gripped the sheets.

"Please what?" Whip lifted his head and looked at the lust-filled face above him.

"Fuck me!" Mitchell screamed when Whip poked his tongue at the wet pucker.

"Here?" Whip grinned. It was great fun to fire up Mitchell.

"God, yes." Mitchell panted and lifted his head with what looked like a great effort. "Please, fill me up with your huge cock. Need it."

"Love it when you talk dirty." It was such a turn-on to have his slightly geeky partner suddenly loosen up.

"You want me to talk dirty?" Mitchell's eyebrows rose.

"Mhm." He stabbed Mitchell's asshole with his tongue, pushing all the way inside this time.

"Fu-uck!" Mitchell pushed back, trying to get more of Whip's tongue inside him. "Driving me crazy here."

"That's the point." Whip grinned and reached over to grab the lube he'd put on the nightstand earlier when they'd unpacked. He was hard enough to stop playing and get to the main event.

"Shit." Mitchell's head dropped back onto the pillow. "Please, just have mercy and fuck me."

He opened the bottle and dribbled some of the cool liquid onto Mitchell's skin. Mitchell hissed, took his knees and pulled them up in an unmistakeable signal. Whip added more lube to his fingers and pushed on in as slowly as possible.

"Yes." Mitchell wiggled his ass. "More."

Whip frowned but decided to trust Mitchell, pushing a second finger in along with the first. He was ready to pull back any time, take it more slowly, but Mitchell moaned with pleasure.

"Love the burn." Mitchell pushed his ass back and forth, fucking himself on Whip's fingers.

He swallowed. That was one of the most erotic things he'd ever seen. He had to grip his own cock with his free hand to stop himself from coming. A few minutes of erotic moaning and creative swearing from Mitchell later, he started to scissor his fingers, then pushed in a third, much to Mitchell's very audible delight.

He'd taken about as much as he could, so he pulled out his fingers, dried them on some convenient tissues—God, how he loved well-stocked guest bedrooms—and grabbed a condom. Seconds later, he was sheathed and kneeling between Mitchell's legs, holding his throbbing cock to his lover's glistening opening.

"Ready?" Whip looked at Mitchell, watching for any sign of hesitance.

"More than." Mitchell pushed down until the tip of Whip's cock had popped into the tight heat. "Fuck me like you mean it, baby."

The pressure around his sensitive cock head and Mitchell's pleading were too much. He grabbed the man's thighs and pushed. Still trying to control the speed, he kept going until he was balls deep.

They both sighed with relief and Mitchell wiggled his ass again. This time, it did all kinds of funny things to Whip's cock.

"Have to move." He could barely hold back.

"Do it! I won't break." Mitchell lifted his hands and held on to Whip's shoulders. "Come on!"

He nodded and pulled back slowly, thrusting forwards as hard as he dared. The feelings coursing through him as he built a rhythm of sensuous in and out only increased the longer he kept up the measured pace. Mitchell looked up at him with enough admiration to make his heart beat even faster.

He quickened his pace and Mitchell howled with joy as his muscles stiffened and he spurted hot semen between their stomachs. The bed only shook slightly this time, but Whip felt it and it encouraged him to speed up. He pounded into the convulsing passage, chasing his own orgasm with all he had. When it boiled up from his balls, raced along his spine and exploded out of his cock, he saw stars from the pleasure.

Still jerking in delicious ecstasy, he collapsed onto Mitchell to catch his breath. Mitchell's arms came up and held him tightly as they both came back down to Earth. He barely had the strength to pull out and deal with the condom and cleanup, but somehow he managed before his final collapse next to Mitchell.

"That was worth the wait." His lover smiled and cuddled into his side.

"Yeah." He still wanted some more hot shower sex with Mitchell, though.

Probably a lot later.

"You have twenty minutes to get across town," Whip said, dropping a kiss on Mitchell's cheek.

"Oh, shit." But Mitchell wasn't talking about the meeting. He was sitting up now, staring at the closed bathroom door. He pointed to the small rivulet of muddy water making its way into the bedroom. "Phillip said we were in danger. Looks like he was right. What the fuck do you suppose that is?"

He stared at the messy, slimy-looking stuff invading their bedroom. He listened, head tilted to catch every sound.

A growling noise from beyond the door seemed to confirm Phillip's point. He looked at Mitchell, but his lover was pale and shrugged, speechless.

"What the hell...? Who the hell is that?" Whip flew from the bed to the bathroom door, but mud flowed around his feet, swirls circling him, sucking him into the floor as they slowed his movements.

Mitchell reached across for him, clever enough to stay on the bed, but the mud was tough. It behaved as if didn't want to let him go, almost like quicksand. Was there such a thing as *quickmud*?

"Hang on to me!" Mitchell shouted, reaching for his hand.

A sinister chuckle from the bathroom made Whip's hair stand on end. He kept struggling, realising that reaching Mitchell was his only hope, but he didn't get anywhere. The mud was too strong and, when he started being pulled under, practically sinking into the floor, he gasped. That should not be possible.

The door creaked open.

Mitchell stared.

Whip swallowed.

The creature was covered in mud, wearing skin-tight swim trunks with an octopus on the crotch. *Ewww!* But that was far from the worst of it. As his gaze slid upwards along the man's body and came to the face, he froze with shock.

"Mudshark!" Whip and Mitchell yelled at the same time.

Mudshark's only reaction was another growl as he flung some more mud into the room. Where was the stuff coming from anyway? As the creature started to march towards Mitchell, his face an angry mask, Whip realised the origins of the mud didn't matter. Mitchell may have been able to hold his own in the arena in their night fights, but since he didn't know how he did it, relying on his abilities was nothing less than careless optimism.

Besides, *this* Mudshark looked a lot stronger, more evil and determined. While his body and face resembled Whip's, there was something about the way he moved and held himself that was different. One angry glare from his eyes made Whip realise he meant business.

Mudshark took another step towards the bed, glaring at Mitchell from red-rimmed eyes, dripping with mud. He completely ignored Whip, who was now halfway submerged in the disgusting quickmud—a substance that didn't seem to bother his alter ego in the least.

Mitchell glared right back and continued to reach for Whip. But, with Mudshark getting closer and Whip sinking by the second, it didn't look as if he was going to be the source of Whip's rescue.

Mudshark's knee hit the bed, leaving ugly brown mud all over the comforter. His big hand encircled Mitchell's arm and he started to pull him off, in the direction of the bathroom.

"What do you want?" Mitchell leant back, resisting the pull.

"You." Mudshark sounded as if he was speaking through a layer of mud, his voice bubbling up from the murky depths.

"Huh?" Mitchell stilled for a moment.

Mudshark immediately took advantage and almost succeeded in pulling him off the bed.

"No way!" Mitchell lifted his free arm, pulling it back and punching Mudshark in the face. His fist slid off the slippery mud.

Mudshark heaved and Mitchell slid right to the edge of the bed.

"Oh, no you don't!" Whip was angry now and redoubled his efforts. Maybe he couldn't get out of the quickmud, but he might be able to move in it, get close enough to intercept his evil twin before he reached the bathroom with Mitchell. Why it was so important he didn't know, but there was something malevolent about this mud. Since its origin seemed to be the bathroom, having Mitchell go in there with Mudshark was not an option.

Mitchell narrowed his eyes and frowned as he concentrated, his entire body vibrating as he focused. A small tremor shook the bed, but didn't get any further. Mitchell tried again. There should have been more of an effect, even if just on the floor and walls of the house, but there was nothing. Shit, the mud must be stopping it. Too bad Mitchell hadn't learned how to consciously control the mud yet.

Mudshark laughed, mumbled something under his breath and punched Mitchell in the face hard enough that he lost consciousness.

"Fuck!" Whip's struggle got frantic. If that barbarian got Mitchell into the bathroom and to the source of the quickmud, his lover would be in major trouble. He should have known better, as he started to sink faster.

Mudshark slung Mitchell over his shoulder as if he weighed nothing and walked back into the bathroom, closing the door behind him. The loud gurgling noise sounded more threatening than the sinister laughter had previously.

The silence that followed was devastating.

Whip pushed hard in one last attempt to get away from the quickmud and almost flew out of the suddenly dry and brittle substance. Regaining his feet, he didn't take the time to catch his breath, raced to the bathroom door and pulled it open with enough force it banged against the wall.

The bathroom was empty.

No Mitchell, and no Mudshark. Just a half-full bathtub of mud, emptying into the drain much too quickly for such a viscous substance. Little green pieces of something dotted the surface.

Mitchell had been kidnapped by God knows who and taken somewhere beyond Whip's reach.

"Fuck!" Whip hit the wall with a balled fist, swearing under his breath when it hurt more than he'd planned. But the pain focused his thoughts enough to realise what had happed. "That bastard used glauconite mixed in with the mud."

It explained how Mudshark had been able to transport Mitchell via mudvortex, since glauconite strengthened existing superpowers. It was also more addictive than cocaine, and its use was illegal.

Why didn't it surprise him that whoever was behind this didn't seem to care?

The bedroom door flew open, hitting the opposite wall, and a very stressed-out Daine raced into the room, followed by Phillip close enough behind to make them look like one person. Both of them were only half dressed, pants clearly pulled on in haste with the buttons still open and shirts askew.

"What's going on? We came as quickly as we could." Daine stared at the bathroom and froze.

"We heard strange noises and—what is that stench?" Phillip wrinkled his nose and frowned as he checked out each corner with squinting eyes. "And where's Mitchell? Wasn't he in here with you?"

"I have no idea what's happening. The stench is from the glauconite-enhanced mud in the bathroom, as far as I can determine, and Mitchell is gone." Whip took a few steps backwards, the full impact of what he'd said only now sinking in. He dropped heavily onto the bed.

"Gone?" Daine's head whipped around as the remaining colour drained from his cheeks.

"Gone." Whip nodded as his stomach roiled. "Kidnapped. And there was absolutely nothing I could do."

"Glauconite?" Phillip's eyebrows were about to take flight, the man looked so shocked. Then he took off into the bathroom almost faster than the eye could follow. "I thought it had been banned from professional fights because it's so addictive."

Daine sat down next to Whip and took his hand. "Don't worry, we'll find him."

"I'm not so sure we can." God, he felt empty all of a sudden." I mean, we don't even know where to look."

"Didn't you see his kidnapper?" Daine's gaze flicked to the bathroom, but Phillip was still gone.

"Yeah, I did." *Nobody will believe me!*

"And you didn't recognise him, is that it?" Daine's full attention returned to Whip. "We can always get an artist to do a facial composite to give to the Marshals."

"The problem is that I *did* recognise him." Whip wished he had the powers to call his lover back. What use were superpowers that couldn't do a thing for him when he needed more than 'normal' support?

"Huh?" Daine shook his head as if to clear it. "You'll have to explain that one to me."

"It was Mudshark." Whip cringed. How could his alter ego have become this independent? And why was his agenda so different from his own? And what the hell did he want with Mitchell?

"Mudshark?" Daine reeled back, letting go of Whip's hand.

"Are you sure?" Phillip stormed out of the bathroom looking furious. Clearly, he had heard everything.

"As sure as I can be. I mean, he was covered in mud, and I was struggling to keep my head above the surface of the damned quickmud at the time, but, yeah, it was definitely Mudshark." Whip felt like hitting something. He needed to get rid of his anger before it consumed him and he did something stupid...like demand they get some glauconite, too, and follow the criminal by creating their own mudvortex.

"Okay, so Mudshark has now acquired the ability to not only leave the fighting pit, but he is also able to follow some pretty detailed instructions." Phillip stated, pacing the room. "On top of which we have a highly illegal substance being used to kidnap people. I checked the bathroom, and while most of the evidence is now gone, I was able to collect a small sample."

"Why?" How was that going to help them?

"Because we'll need proof to convince the authorities that what's going on here is serious."

Phillip leaned against a wall and rubbed his temples. "The only problem is that I have no idea whom we can trust. Either Mr. Damek or Judge Lashdown would be the logical first choice, but after the way they pushed Mitchell into the last fight, I'm not so sure they are not involved, or at the very least affected. And if the Judge has been compromised, who is to say that the whole Earth Court system isn't corrupt by now?"

"We need to find Mitchell first, anyway. Who knows what they're doing to him? We can't just let them keep him and not do something to try to stop them!" Whip almost hoped it was 'only' another fight. But there was always the possibility of blackmail. After all, Whip was a renowned wrestler and they could easily get to him by using Mitchell. He could only hope whoever was behind this hadn't figured out how close Mitchell and he had become.

"If we want to find Mitchell, we'll have to figure out who is behind this whole debacle." Daine tilted his head. "Who would gain from having Mitchell under their control?"

"That's just it. I have no idea." Whip felt like pacing as well, but the room really was too small for that. "The obvious suspect is whoever is behind all these underground fights. Lots of money is involved there, and if they could get Mitchell to fight for them on an ongoing basis, what with all his newfound superpowers, that could be quite profitable for them."

"I bet you Friday Otis Doombringer could help. He must know something—why else would he have been hiding for so long?" Daine frowned. "Do you think we could ask the trolls and risi to help us find him? They are in charge of the Witness Trollection Programme, after all."

"I agree. We should get them to start looking. They seem to be immune from this split personality issue, as far as we can see, and they have widespread connections all over the planet via their underground tunnel and cave systems." Phillip nodded and stopped away from the wall.

"Isn't there someone who can help us track Mitchell from here? I mean, this is where he vanished and there must be some sort of trace?" It seemed like the most obvious solution to him.

"Normally that would be the task of an Earth Marshal, but I have no idea how to find one who is honest." Phillip scratched his head.

"I bet you Ty Anglin would know." Daine grinned when Phillip slapped his forehead. "He may be a Water Marshal, but I'm sure he has enough connections to the other Houses to be able to tell us who is trustworthy."

"Why didn't I think of that?" Phillip walked over to Daine and kissed him enthusiastically on the lips.

"That's why you keep me around." Dane grinned.

"What's going on around here?" Alicia rolled her wheelchair about halfway in the door, looking sleepy as if she had taken a nap. "Where is Mitchell?"

"Um..." Whip didn't want to have to explain Mitchell's disappearance to his sister, but it didn't look as if he had any choice. So he told an increasingly agitated Alicia the whole story.

"Well!" Alicia looked more upset than shocked. "I only have two things to say. Njáll better help us on this one and I think it's time we get some real help."

"You're not even shocked about the whole superpowers thing?" Whip squinted at her. "You knew, didn't you? But how? Mitchell had no idea!"

"Yeah, well, we don't have time to go into all of this now. We can talk about it later. Now we need to focus on getting my brother back." She drummed her fingers on the top of an armrest, scrunching her forehead in thought.

"And how do you suggest we do that?" Whip was quite impressed with how well she had taken the news and more than curious what she would come up with to help them find a solution. An additional point of view could never hurt.

"The whole situation just strikes me as too coincidental. I mean, we have this huge upswing of wrestling — mud-wrestling to be precise — then Mitchell gets hired by WWW and ends up in a few fights. Illegal ones, no less. At the same time we have Whip here facing his evil twin, or whatever, and other indications that all is not as it should be in the Earth House, including even the legal system." She took a deep breath and looked at each of them before continuing. "I think there is something fundamentally wrong with the whole Earth House and, since we have no way of fixing it, it's time we get some help from the outside."

"You mean the other Houses?" Whip wasn't sure they'd be happy to get involved — superpower traditions were pretty much about divide and conquer.

"That would be one option." Alicia nodded. "But the political pain to get them to agree on anything, never mind the battles about jurisdiction, would take longer than Mitchell has. No, what I mean is going back to the very fundamentals of the Earth Power. The parts that are the oldest and least likely to be affected by the current mess, because they are immune to all the power-wrangling."

"Are you talking about the Hephaestos family?" Phillip nodded slowly. "That could work."

"That is brilliant." Whip wished he would have thought of that. "They go back so far that some say they and their powers, so closely linked to lava, should be part of the Fire House, but for whatever reason they often side with Earth."

"It makes sense if you think about it. Cold lava turns into earth and fertile ground for growing plants eventually, so a lot of their work and powers are much more closely linked to Earth." Alicia waved a hand. "Not that it matters, really, since what we need them for is help in understanding the current problem or sickness in the younger parts of the Earth House, and they may just know how to help figure out what is going on."

"And I bet you my father knows exactly whom to talk to." Daine grinned. "He isn't one of the most powerful and well-connected Fire Mages around for nothing, after all."

"Okay, we have a plan." Whip felt a lot better. The urgency of finding Mitchell hadn't lessened, but at least they had some options now. The need to find his lover grew with every second, and he was damned if he was going to sit around for another moment. He jumped up. "Let's start making some calls!"

Chapter Eight

Mitchell opened his eyes to complete darkness. Not just blinds-stopping-light-from-getting-into-the-bedroom darkness, but the absolute black of...nothingness. Was that even a word?

He was still naked and too cold for comfort. He took a deep breath and winced at the pain on the left side of his body. Trying to sit up hurt and what was it going to get him anyway? It wasn't as if he could walk out of here. There wasn't anywhere to walk to that he could see, and without knowing exactly what he was facing, he'd be stupid to start running around. He fell back to the hard rock he was lying on and started to consider his options.

Opening his eyes wider and hoping he'd get used to the darkness, maybe discover a shard of light somewhere, was useless. He'd need to use his other senses to figure out where the hell he was and how to get back to Whip. They'd had such a great time, finally, even if he suspected the cupcakes Daine had brought contained some sort of aphrodisiac. Why else had they all suddenly been so horny?

Then the creature, one that looked an awful lot like yet another incarnation of Mudshark, had come along, torn him from the bed and dragged him off into the bathroom. Poor Whip had been trying to fight the strangely alive mud that was holding him rooted to the spot, but to no avail. God, he hoped his lover was okay.

As for the rest of the trip—he'd rather not remember diving into the mud-filled bathtub, being dragged under and feeling as if he was being pulled through the drain. He'd have sworn there was no such thing as a mudvortex but that was exactly what it had felt like. And the stench? Gah, close to unbearable. The fumes alone would be a very effective ingredient for stench warfare, that was for sure.

Whatever that stuff was, it had been part of the crazy mud mixture in the bathtub and he'd bet it had something to do with the fact that he had, apparently, travelled by mud.

To this place.

Wherever 'this place' was.

The vague stench of the mud still stuck to him, so his sense of smell wouldn't be the key to figuring out what was going on. Since it was so dark and didn't feel like a confined space, it made him think that he was probably in some underground cave. The air was damp and there was a sound of dripping water in the distance.

The cave theory sounded more likely by the second. Why would anyone put him here, though? Why not kick him into another mudpit to fight? That had been the MO so far, but apparently whoever was behind the mysterious goings-on had changed tactics. Or someone else had joined the 'let's get Mitchell and Whip party' and had stashed him away. Were they hiding him? Keeping him prisoner? Trying to intimidate him?

All very real possibilities, but he wouldn't find out by remaining where he was and taking a nap.

The dripping water got louder. Or maybe his hearing was improving because there were no other sounds. Now it was coming closer. What the hell?

He sat up, ignoring the flare of pain from his side — which must have come from some sort of bruise by the feel of it — and stretched his arms to his sides. If he could find a wall, he might be able to follow it and find out what shape and size this cave was.

Of course, there was nothing within his reach. That would have been too easy. He felt along the floor instead, deciding he had been placed on some kind of rock. Reaching farther into the darkness he found a ridge, which he determined, by following it with his hands, went all the way around him in a rectangular shape, about a foot high and encircling a space about the size of a bed.

The rock on his side of the weird enclosure was smooth. The other side was rough and there were a few protrusions on the floor just outside of where he was that felt like stalagmites.

"Ouch! Shit!" The little buggers were quite sharp. He put his bleeding finger into his mouth, not knowing what else to do to stop the bleeding.

The dripping sound got louder again. It came from somewhere on his left. Some sort of wave lapping against the edge of a pool, or a lake, made his heart rate increase. The soft breath, almost a moan, jolted him fully awake.

"Fuck!" There was something out there, and he had no idea if it was friend or foe, couldn't see a thing and was completely helpless.

"Language, language," said a gruff voice from far below.

It sounded vaguely familiar to him, but he couldn't put a face to it. He stopped struggling for a moment. Actual terror had started to grip him. He'd gone straight back in time to the moment his mother had strapped him into the back of the car, Alicia snuggled beside him.

Tears rolled down his cheeks as he remembered. There'd been no such thing as special child safety seats back then, but his mother had put seatbelts around both of them. Her demeanour had been so odd...so...off.

"We're going for a little ride," she said. He could see his mother's face as clearly as if it were happening to him now. He'd been scared but had said nothing. The awful memory unspooled in his mind like a movie — a memory he hadn't even known he had.

But that was why he'd gone to see Carrie Hoffman, the soul retriever. He'd wanted his memories back. She'd said he'd regain his life power — his will to live.

He watched, his horror mounting as his mother screamed in frustration. She could become violent if you argued or didn't instantly comply with her demands. Mitchell had suffered her stinging, wicked facial slaps on more than one occasion. He'd even taken beatings for Alicia, who'd cried often under their mother's cruel hand.

He said nothing, though his mother had strapped him in tight. He could smell the booze on her breath. He averted his gaze since she was wild-eyed and increasingly furious.

"Buckle the bitch in," she said of Alicia.

Bitch? Mitchell was so afraid of his mother in that moment. He buckled his toddler sister in but the nozzle on the belt had rusted and wouldn't comply. His mother screamed, whacked his head and, mercifully, the belt slid into place. He saw stars as his mother backed out of the car.

People came running.

"Don't do this, Kathy," someone said.

Another voice. His father. "Not my babies! You can't take my babies!"

His mother slammed the back door. She screamed at Mitchell's father. She began to slap him. Mitchell had forgotten that. His mother regularly hit his father. Sometimes, after they'd both had a few beers, they argued. She'd strike him...lash out. His father would leave until tempers cooled off...and she'd take her aggressions out on Mitchell.

Mitchell would never forget the look on his father's face when he tried to open the back door. Mitchell stared at him, frightened now. Alicia wailed beside him.

"Look after your sister," his father said.

"Help me!" Mitchell couldn't believe his father wasn't trying to get his own children out of the car.

A few of the neighbours – the doorman, too – were trying to talk his mother into not driving away.

"You're angry," one of the women who lived in the building said. "Don't take it out on the children!"

Mitchell started to cry. His mother swore and yelled at everyone and stepped on the gas. Too late, his father started running after the car. Mitchell was horrified when Alicia's seatbelt pinged right out of the buckle. He did his best to hold her back, to keep her in place. His mother accelerated. His father slipped away from them.

She stopped. She was panting and crying as his father came to the driver's side window. He was talking to her.

"Give me the keys, Kathy."

She sat at the wheel, head bent.

Mitchell couldn't see through his tears. Poor Alicia was a tiny wreck beside him. She wanted to be held and comforted. He wanted to scream, "No!" He loved Alicia. He could *never deny her affection. He was the one who held her through the nights when she couldn't sleep.*

He tried to keep her back in her seat because his mother was in a rage the likes of which he'd never seen. He knew she was going to kill them.

It all happened so fast. His father, who'd never been able to read his wife's moods accurately, was talking in a soothing voice.

"We can work it out, baby," he said.

She suddenly put the car in reverse and drove backwards very quickly. Mitchell put a protective arm across Alicia's wriggling body. He glanced up to see his mother shift gears. She stepped on the gas. His father, now ahead of them, saw her coming for him. He started to run, but she clipped him. He still got away, screaming. Police sirens blared.

Alicia howled with fear now, jumping into Mitchell's arms.

"It's okay, he said against his little sister's soft cheek. But it wasn't. His mother slammed into his father, his body crumpling under the vehicle. She reversed and drove over him before driving off. She was laughing like a hyena as she sped down the street...straight into a lamp post.

Alicia flew out of Mitchell's arms and through the windshield. Mitchell was pinned against the front seat, which had jammed up against him. Then he lost consciousness.

"Stop crying," the voice below him ordered.

Mitchell couldn't help it.

"Mom?" he whispered.

* * * *

Whip had never been anywhere close to the legendary Hephaestos family. He'd heard of them and had wondered about them since their business supplied all the metal goods used in the Elementals' sports activities. They provided javelins and anvils, pre-charged with superpowers, for major contests. They supplied steel and copper tips for archery contests. They called themselves blacksmiths and belonged to the House of Fire but were considered the closest thing to supernatural royalty.

Part of the reason was that Copper Hephaestos was one of the oldest living humans at the age of one hundred and seventy-five. Not that normal humans even knew he existed. He was said to have been descended from the very gods of Mount Olympus. In fact, he was said to have a direct lineage to Hephaestus, the Greek god of fire, volcanoes, technology, craftsmen, sculptors, artisans, blacksmiths, metals and metallurgy.

He had so many intriguing characteristics peculiar to the god that nobody disputed his lineage. Like Hephaestus, Copper Hephaestos was drop-dead handsome, even at his very ripe old age, but he, too, was lame. All his power and abilities had never been able to help him walk right. However, he didn't let it stop him. As a young man, he'd married the gorgeous Ember, a young sculptress from the Fire House who, like her husband, looked amazing even though she was one hundred and fifty years old.

Their union was by all accounts not only joyous but they had produced three remarkable children who, in an unusual set of circumstances, had each displayed abilities and affinities for the other three elemental superpower houses. Their daughter Shula had defied the Arabic definition of her birth name — meaning fire — by becoming an active Earth House participant. Their eldest son Cinder was a Water man, and their youngest son Aden was an Air Mage.

And so Mr. and Mrs. Hephaestos never took sides in matters of business and politics. They could be counted upon to be fair, honest…and impartial.

The small group that now congregated at Mitchell's residence consisted of Njáll and Alicia, who seemed quite lovey-dovey, Whip, Daine and Phillip. They'd been joined by Daine's father Marcel, a Fire House judge, and his lover Christopher, a Fire Mage and also Daine's business partner.

Whip had met Marcel a few times at Fabulous Cupcakes and never ceased to be amazed that the grumpy-looking, mercurial judge could have landed such an all-out hottie like Christopher.

The two men seemed madly in love, though, and as if by unspoken agreement, the judge seemed to have taken charge.

"Are were ready to go visit the famous first family of Fire?" he asked, a small smile playing on his lips.

Whip nodded. He was grateful that Marcel Paradis had arrived as soon as he'd heard there was a problem. It irked him terribly that Goyathlay Damek, the Earth House attorney, had not responded to Whip's messages and neither had the Earth judge, Early Lashdown.

Justice Paradis had deemed it necessary to contact them and give them a chance to explain themselves. Both had ignored all efforts to speak to them. Maybe they were busy protecting Friday's ass. Whip sure hoped so. He expected Damek at least to have a damned good reason for not being here when he'd been issued an official Superpower Interlocutory Order.

"I think we will be able to talk to Mr. and Mrs. Hephaestos quite easily. This was an inspired suggestion, Phillip," Justice Paradis said after they'd all waited for a good twenty minutes for replies from the Earth attorney and judge.

Whip got a kick out of the smile Daine shot his lover. Usually it was Phillip who listened to praise being heaped on Daine.

"Where do they live?" Whip asked.

"Mount Olympus," Christopher responded.

"Really?"

"Mount Olympus in Los Angeles."

Everybody laughed. It eased the tension somewhat then they were back to business again.

"We'll need a bullet train," Justice Paradis said, glancing down at Njáll. "But please, make it a nice-smelling one, Commander Jørgensen. I abhor bad odours."

The king of the trolls looked miffed but pulled himself together. They all walked down the hill back to Union Square where he proudly conjured one on to the train tracks.

Huh. I see the judge gets a fancy-schmancy bullet train. Mitchell and I get the dregs of the fleet...

Just thinking Mitchell's name made Whip worry. It had been a long time since he'd allowed anyone close enough to him to care about their well-being. He took comfort in knowing whoever had Mitchell would keep him alive for a battle in the mudpit. If and when that happened, Whip would be there by his side.

I want to be the first person in his life who actually works to protect him.

He watched the tender way Njáll buckled Alicia into the seat reserved for disabled passengers. Her face shone at the little man's attention. Whip had never seen the disabled seating feature before because he didn't know any disabled people in the world of superpowers. He had a sneaking feeling that Alicia would soon be walking if what he'd heard about Ember Hephaestos was true.

Whip thought about her husband Copper, and how all his power had not been able to help his lame leg. Whip looked forward to meeting the couple.

He was astonished to find that what seemed like seconds later they had arrived at Hollywood and Highland train station in Los Angeles. They trooped out, Njáll leading the way.

"I have arranged for ground transportation!" he shouted, his hands reaching up to push Alicia's chair. She was a feisty little thing, however, and insisted on propelling herself.

Njáll seemed to like that. "What a woman!" he chortled, winking at Whip as he took the elevator to the street with Alicia.

Whip and the others took the escalator. As they tumbled out onto the busy intersection of Hollywood and Highland, Whip blinked at the harsh light and the absolute mayhem on the street. People were shoving one another, fighting to get near a plethora of entertainers outside Grauman's Chinese Theater.

Now that he focused on the chaos, it seemed the entertainers were trying to coerce the tourists into paying a buck for photos they didn't want to take. Dressed up to look like movie characters, the performers represented dozens of famous personalities. Darth Vader and Johnny Depp's Captain Jack from *The Pirates of the Caribbean* movie series were in an animated conversation with each other. Movie villain Freddy Krueger was very popular, probably because the so-called Canadian Psycho, a serial killer who'd been arrested in Belgium, had posted online photos of himself with the character on a trip to Hollywood.

A man dressed as Gene Simmons in full KISS regalia might have been okay if he'd had the right tongue moves. Homer Simpson seemed to sweat through his spongy costume. Whip was shocked to see somebody dressed as Mudpit Madman, Mitchell's mudwrestling character.

Daine and Christopher turned to Whip in unison, sympathy in their eyes.

"We're going to find him," Daine said, pushing past the throng of humanity to touch Whip's shoulder. A funny little man stood wearing a balaclava stood at the side of the road. He looked like a troll but Whip wasn't sure since he was otherwise dressed as a mini replica Madman in a red swimsuit and leather boots.

He ushered the small party onboard a white minibus, waving away an Asian family that first tried following them then started snapping photos.

Daine, Christopher, Whip and Njáll lifted Alicia's chair onto the bus.

The man in the red suit jumped into the driver's seat and angled into traffic, narrowly missing colliding into a city bus. He drove like a maniac along Hollywood Boulevard at a dizzying pace, zigzagging between vehicles.

"Hey!" Justice Paradis shouted. "Where's the fire?" He would have fallen out of his seat had his handsome lover Christopher not plucked at his shirt collar and yanked him back into place.

The others let loose with a few choice remarks, too. Njáll stood protective guard over Alicia, who stared up at him adoringly from her strapped-in wheelchair, as if she knew, just knew, the little man would let no harm befall her.

For the first time in his life, Whip began to dread speed. He closed his eyes. The bus lurched as they made a sharp right turn uphill. Whip opened his eyes again as they barrelled up Laurel Canyon and made another sharp right through a massive stone arch engraved with the words *Mount Olympus*.

A hush fell over the group as they entered the mountainside enclave of big, expensive houses set into the dramatic peaks of the Hollywood Hills. The driver plunged left and along a tiny, circular road that Whip thought would need to be navigated carefully since it had no guardrail. One wrong move could send them over the edge of the ravine and into the canyons below. Whip kept glimpsing backyards and blue swimming pools as the bus zoomed up the steep, increasingly narrow road. They came to the top of the crest and a huge, stunning metal guard gate.

The occupants of the bus stared at the ornate work that looked like a blend of metals — the kind a god of blacksmiths would create.

What was odd, however, was that the gates seemed to be guarding a sharp drop into the hills. There was nothing ahead of it.

"Holy fuck!" Whip rushed forwards and stared out the window. He sensed that something gorgeous and stunning lay on the other side of the gates. Even though he was of the superpowers world, he didn't yet have permission to enter so the property was protected from view.

The others soon joined him.

"Can you see anything?" they all asked each other.

"Back off!" the driver said as a voice spoke from a metallic box at the guard gate.

"Who are you?" it demanded.

The driver lowered his window with the press of a button. "Erm—" he said then shot a desperate look over his shoulder at the occupants surrounding him.

"Wait!" Justice Paradis held up his hand. "We have royalty on board. I do think Commander Jørgensen should speak for us all."

"I should say so!" Njáll huffed, elbowing them all aside.

"This is Njáll. Royal Troll Squad Commander Jørgensen here to see the king and queen," he announced.

The Hephaestoses went by Mr. and Mrs. but were, as Whip knew, considered royalty. They would appreciate the Commander's respectful introduction.

A few seconds later, Whip felt a rush of heat and looked out the window. His gasps matched the others' as an astonishing palace emerged — a fairy palace that seemed built of fire and lava stone. It glistened like a dark jewel. The bus lurched forwards then dropped, shaking the passengers who grabbed onto whatever they could to steady themselves as the vehicle fell onto a pair of narrow metal rods that glided them across a cavernous drop. The bus stopped just outside the entrance.

The bus driver opened the door. Sweat beaded on his lip and brow.

"You want me to wait?" he asked. He looked petrified.

"Of course we do," Justice Paradis said, he and Njáll fighting each other to leave the bus first.

The bus driver swallowed.

"We won't be long," Whip said. "Thank you for getting us here safely." As the others left the bus, he said, "Don't look down."

The driver nodded, looking very pale.

Whip joined the others outside as the doors to the palace opened and an incredibly beautiful woman, with Titian-coloured hair, a long tunic and matching pants of the same hue as her hair, came to greet them.

Her voice was husky, yet musical. Every man standing before her seemed intoxicated.

"Commander Jørgensen," she said, a smile upon her lovely face. Most of the men present, except Njáll, were gay but there was no denying the allure the woman had over them. "Such a pleasure to meet you," she said, extending both hands to Njáll. He jumped right into her open arms as she bent to him and hugged her waist.

She laughed.

"Mrs. Hephaestos, we've come on a most urgent matter," Marcel said.

Njáll kept hugging the woman, much to Alicia's chagrin.

"Please, come inside, and do call me Ember," she insisted. "Mrs. Hephaestos makes me feel so old."

As she led them along a sparkling gold corridor, Njáll still attached to her hip, Alicia wheeled herself beside Whip.

"She doesn't have a line on her face."

Alicia was right. Ember Hephaestos was astonishing. He liked her little joke about her age, but Alicia looked worried.

"Njáll's just infatuated," he told her.

Alicia looked at Whip, misery in her gaze. "If you say so. Whip…I don't want to lose my brother. He's always taken care of me. You think she can help us?"

"I hope so, sweetie." He pushed her along, Alicia not complaining for once. They arrived at an old-fashioned-looking parlour with black and white floor tiles. A man who was tall and movie-star handsome, yet sporting a pronounced limp, came to greet them.

Everything in the room had been delicately wrought from metal, yet the cushions and pillows on each available surface gave the appearance of lush comfort.

"Who is this exquisite creature?" Ember's gaze fell on Alicia. "My darling child." Ember knelt before her. "Why did nobody bring you to me sooner?" Her eyes filled with tears.

All the men in the room seemed emotional as the two women spoke.

"Because I never knew you existed," Alicia said.

"Copper!" Ember's husband limped over to her side. "Darling, please help me carry her."

"Carry her?" Njáll seemed apoplectic. "Carry her where?"

Marcel put a hand on the little man's shoulder. Everybody watched as Ember and Copper lifted Alicia from her chair and carried her across the room in their arms.

Ember glanced at Marcel Paradis. "Can you bring a goblet of wine, please?"

The judge nodded. Evidently he'd been here before because he hurried to the golden sideboard without hesitation and picked up a decanter of ruby-red wine. He removed the gold and metal top. It came loose with a pop. He poured some into a golden goblet and replaced the decanter. He followed Ember and Copper, beckoning the others with his free hand. They all stuck to his heels. In a sumptuous room carpeted in a thick, fire-coloured carpet, the couple put Alicia onto a golden throne.

So, it's true. The Throne of Thanatos *exists!*

Whip felt like a little kid. His mother had read him the stories as a child. He'd thought it was a myth. He glanced at Ember, who knelt at Alicia's feet, holding the goblet up to Alicia's mouth.

I thought she *was a myth…*

He wondered if Alicia had any clue what was about to happen to her.

Marcel Paradis waited a goodly minute before he spoke. He, too, was aware of the momentous occasion in Alicia Dykins' life, but another life hung in the balance.

"Ember, Copper, we have a problem." He quickly launched into an explanation of everything that had happened.

"So that's why nobody brought her to us before?" Copper Hephaestos looked very angry. "Come, my child," he said, holding his hand down to Alicia.

She glanced up from the wine in her cup. "I need my wheelchair," she said.

Ember stood on her other side. "No you don't, my darling. Take his hand."

"But I can't." Alicia trembled.

"It's all right, gel," Njáll said, rushing to Alicia's feet. She glanced at everyone, saw the encouraging smiles. She looked up at Ember, who took the goblet.

"You must trust me, child. Take my husband's hand."

Alicia did as she was told. Copper was very gentle with her. He helped Alicia to her feet. Only when she'd taken a few steps and he released her to walk on her own did the young woman look at them all.

"I can stand," she said, sobs racking her body. "Oh my God. I can feel my legs!" She took a few more steps. Her face crumpled in distress. "Oh, Mitchell! Why aren't you here to see this?"

* * * *

"Mitchypooooooo!"

Mitchell lay on the rock, the spooky voice from below taunting him. It was a strange-sounding intonation. Alternating between male and female, he thought at first it was his mother then mentally chided himself for such foolish thoughts.

She was a monster. The only one he knew…well, until he'd started meeting some of the freaks and weirdoes he'd encountered in the world of the elemental superpowers. He shut his mind to the memory of the manic leer on Justice Lashdown's face as he had pushed Mitchell down into the mudpit.

Mitchell suddenly relaxed. Something had upset the person below him. He could hear him/her whispering, agitated. What had gone wrong?

He heard two words. *They know.*

Who knew what? Mitchell felt a calm envelop him. His entire life he'd been depressed. He'd fought turning into the kind of beast his mother had been. Each and every day he'd worked to be a tireless caretaker for Alicia. A friend to those who needed one. And yet, he realised now, he'd kept people at arm's length, especially men. His past lovers had accused him of being distant. One had even said he was frigid. He smiled, thinking of his ardent lovemaking with Whip.

Oh, I am far from frigid. He found himself chuckling.

"He's laughing," said a male voice from the depths below.

"Quiet!" shrieked the male/female voice.

Mitchell's old childhood fear rose to the surface. His mother used to go berserk when he disobeyed her. He'd always tried to give her respect. He did anything he could to avoid a beating. However, it wasn't always easy when she issued a command followed by a contradictory order.

Pain and terror quaked through his body.

"I'm here," said a voice in his head.

Holy heck! It was his uncle.

He felt himself immobilised by crippling paralysis. This was what had led him to Carrie Hoffman. For weeks he'd had nightmares, accompanied by this strange sensation of being stuck. He focused on breathing and hoped his earlier peacefulness would return.

It all became clear to him now. Because he'd resisted being close to men, he'd missed the connectedness he'd so desperately yearned for. Turning thirty had been pure torture. He felt he'd never meet a man. He'd stayed alive for his sister because she needed him. But all the years of blocking out men who might have been suitable partners had been, he realised now, a futile attempt at blocking the part of himself that resembled his mother.

If he let go of his control, bad things would happen. He would become a monster.

He'd let go with Whip and had discovered...a world of joy and happiness. Hope. He'd discovered the inklings of love.

And his own power to make earthquakes. He could hear Whip and Alicia talking in his head now. What was going on? It was as if they were all on a merry-go-round in his mind. He couldn't stop it.

"Be careful," a voice warned. Daine Paradis.

"I'm here," said another.

Whip!

The warm, squishy, peaceful feeling enveloped him again. *He's thinking about me.* He smiled. He couldn't help it. Just thinking about Whip made him want to be happy.

"Why's he smiling?" the male/female voice below said, a trifle louder.

"Give him something to smile about," the male voice said.

Mitchell heard their weird, terrifying, ice-cold laughter. He shifted, the tethered fingers of his left hand scratching against a jagged stalagmite. He could smell blood. His blood.

"Mitchypooooooo!"

The voice sounded closer.

There had been times Mitchell had dreamt of death. Times when he'd contemplated suicide. He had never gone through with it for the sake of Alicia. He didn't want her to be completely orphaned. He didn't want her to live without love. Without his help. He had a sudden flash of her walking.

It had been so good to see her on her feet in the mudpit.

I miss her. I love her.

He felt the person coming closer but didn't hear footsteps. Rather, he heard a strange gliding, a strong muddy odour permeating the air. He was surprised when he saw a shimmer of scaly skin. Something slid over him.

Mitchell stared as the gigantic snake-like creature made its slow way across his belly. He heard footsteps from his left and a plop on his right as the creature slithered off the rock beside him.

"Miss me?" a female voice said.

Mitchell gazed to his right. The giant snake-like creature was, he knew, a Mongolian death worm. He knew this without benefit of ever having seen one before. He looked into the leering, ugly face that hovered over him, rising like a cobra head.

"Not really, Mom," he said.

Chapter Nine

Mitchell saw the fury in the creature's eyes. He had no idea how to fight her since he'd never stood up to her as a kid, but she screamed, a long, ear-shattering sound that made the man standing beside Mitchell duck for cover.

Larry Parker! His boss!

"What are you doing here?" Mitchell asked.

Larry hid behind a huge rock, covering his ears.

Mitchell was livid now. The hideous worm draped herself across him. He knew she would squeeze him to death. Her disgusting, scaly body kept wrapping around him.

Oh, no, I'm not dying this way.

He summoned all his anger and the earth shook.

"Earthquake!" Larry Parker shrieked like a girl.

The death worm kept twisting itself around Mitchell. The man who hadn't wanted to be alive now didn't want to die. In his mind's eye he saw Alicia, Whip, Foti...a circle of friends...a woman with hair the colour of fire. Who was she?

Rage bubbled from him like nothing he'd ever experienced and the walls came tumbling down.

The death worm hissed, blood oozing from gaping wounds. He/she/it slithered away from him and over to Larry Parker. She crawled up his leg, seeking solace.

"Make it stop!" Larry screamed.

Mitchell made it stop as soon as he'd freed his arms and legs. His left hand hurt. The bindings had cut him deeply but he didn't care. He had to leave here. He had to get away. The earth stopped rumbling, stones and rocks stopped falling. He stood on shaky legs, his head spinning. The death worm changed into a female form. She didn't look like his mother...

Oh, no. It's the girl Larry had brought to the meeting with him in New York!

Mitchell shook his head. Bewitchment. That's what it was.

"How do you two know each other?" Mitchell asked as Larry put his arm around her. The girl moaned, and when she turned to Mitchell she had his mother's face.

"She seduced me," Larry said.

"That explains a lot." Mitchell couldn't resist the sarcastic tone. He had to keep them talking long enough to give him time for figuring a way out of here. He was naked and alone...but at least he wasn't scared anymore.

"She did." Larry coughed, trying to sit up now. "She turned up at my offices one day. A beautiful sylph of a girl."

Mitchell glanced at the female body that was struggling, it seemed, between the pretty young thing in a slip-dress, Mitchell's mother and the hideous worm.

Mitchell couldn't stop staring. He had never seen anything or anyone quite so revolting.

"You tortured me all my life," he said. "You killed my father and you crippled my sister."

"You were adopted!" his mother hissed.

"No, I wasn't. You have power. As does Foti...and as do I. How did Alicia not...?" The truth hit him. Hard.

"My God. She's the one who was adopted!" He hated his mother more than ever now. *Hated* her for her constant lies and torment.

"How does Foti figure into this?" His mind raced but he couldn't figure out how kind and loving Foti could be this monster's sister.

"He was supposed to kill you. I bewitched him too." The female figure began changing into the scaly worm form again.

"You sent him to us two years ago...as a *hit man*?"

Mitchell might have been new to all the superpowers stuff but he recalled so many things Whip had told him and pieces, like long-hidden puzzle scraps, finally fell into place. Whatever his mother had attempted, Foti had not given in to her attempts to take over his mind and soul. He'd left the underground world he'd dominated...and had protected Alicia and Mitchell.

Hadn't he?

Of course he had. There were many times Foti could have killed either one of them quickly...easily. But he hadn't. His powers had lain dormant until recently.

What had tipped him off? It must have been that call. But who had it been from?

He remembered now. Foti had received a call from Damek, the Earth House attorney. Mitchell didn't trust the guy, or the Earth House judge. A long history with an abusive mother would do that to a guy. His mother had returned from the dead...somehow — if she'd really died at all — and invaded the body of Larry's young paramour. She'd infiltrated Foti's mud fight a couple of years ago and killed his opponent.

She came back to finish us all off.

Mitchell glanced at her. She had wrapped herself around Larry's throat, squeezing the life out of him. The man's eyes and tongue bugged out.

"I'm. Still. Gorgeous!" the worm shouted as she squeezed out the last breath from Larry Parker. He stopped fighting her, his vacant eyes staring ahead. The dripping sound Mitchell had heard returned now with a vengeance. Something plopped on his head. Mitchell looked up. A huge snake-like creature was slithering down the canyon towards him.

Water was dripping faster now but the huge wormy thing had all his attention.

Holy shit! It's Foti!

"Don't be afraid," his uncle warned.

But Mitchell *was* afraid. He had two of them after him now. He glanced at his mother.

She'd vanished.

Mitchell didn't know where to turn...what to do. He focused on his rage...all that he had inside him. A minor rumble and the earth cracked. He heard his mother's scream of frustration. He glanced down, surprised to see she'd materialised beside him. She lunged for his ankle. Mitchell jumped. He didn't think twice. He'd rather brave the unknown than certain death at her mercy.

He'd always been afraid of heights. Come to think of it, he'd been afraid of *everything*.

Now he was plummeting to the depths of the cave. He braced himself, panic gripping his heart. Beneath him, water churned and he landed feet first in it.

He was shocked at how cold it was, the chill soaring through him. When he fought the murky depths and came to the surface he was pleased and gulped deep breaths even though the air was fetid. He glanced upwards and saw his mother and Foti gazing over the rock edge down at him.

Mitchell would have said something had a giant wave not washed over him and carried him away. Over and over he rolled. He couldn't breathe. The dirty water swirled around him. He thought he'd lost consciousness but it was only his sense of direction that had vanished. There was no up or down and his body protested the lack of oxygen.

Oddly, he'd never been afraid of the water. He clawed at the seaweed tumbling around his body. He propelled himself upwards.

He was in the ocean. In the middle of nowhere. Each way he turned, he saw nothing but waves.

On and on…nothing but ocean.

I'll never make it out of here alive…

* * * *

Whip and Mitchell were sitting side by side on a golden beach. Mitchell was naked beside him, laughing up at the sun. Whip, too, was naked and he leaned into the man he now cherished, kissing him. Their tongues met, their lips locking fiercely. There was nothing gentle in their embrace. Sheer, raw need.

The maleness of Mitchell was intoxicating.

"Should we be doing this?" Mitchell asked. "Somebody might see."

"I don't care." And he didn't. Whip pushed Mitchell back against the warm sand, the fine grains dusting his lover's shoulders and glistening arms. Whip kissed him, Mitchell's hips arching up. Whip laughed and moved down Mitchell's body, capturing his cock with his mouth, hungry for a taste.

Ember's voice intruded the gauzy vision in his mind. "Focus, Whip."

Whip came back to reality. He was sitting on Ember's golden throne. Daine stood beside her and took a plate from Whip's hand. Whip didn't remember much beyond the first bite of mudpie. It had sent his spirits…his whole being…into orbit.

"Drink this." Ember's voice was soft but commanding.

"Hmph?" Whip wanted to be back on the sand with Mitchell.

She pressed a goblet into his hands. He sipped the warm red wine and slumped, relaxing against the precious metal of the throne. People whispered around him but he didn't listen. They all paced, probably worried about Mitchell, just as he was.

In his mind, he tried to go back to the dream. But it was like every wonderful dream he'd ever had. Once awakened, he could never go back.

Oh…no…*there it is!* For a moment, he glimpsed…no, he could taste the salty sweetness of Mitchell's cock. He could feel the man's arms pulling him closer, tighter.

"I want you, Whip."

He gulped. The dream changed. Oh…no. They weren't together anymore. Mitchell was far away from him. Whip called and called his lover's name, but Mitchell was carried away by a brutal wave.

"Where are you?" Ember asked. Whip was vaguely aware of the immediate silence in the room.

"He's at the beach." Whip could see him clearly. "No. Not a beach. The ocean. He's stuck in the middle of the ocean."

"Can you see where?"

"No." Whip tuned into his lover's fear as he turned in every direction. "He can't see land. He's scared." Whip watched Mitchell's beautiful face. "He's escaped the monsters."

"Monsters?" Ember sounded startled. "There's more than one?"

"Friday." Whip began to gasp. The water Mitchell was treading was frigid. It was as if the chill pressed on his lungs.

"We need that Water Marshal. What's his name?" Marcel Paradis asked.

"Ty Anglin," Whip said, desperate to yank Mitchell to the beautiful dream Ember had given him of the two of them. For one brief moment, Whip had been able to communicate telepathically with Mitchell. Something had separated their shared mental space.

Terror. I could feel his terror.

Whip sat in the chair as calls were made. Everybody had cell phones going—landlines, too. It had always struck Whip as so strange that there wasn't a Batphone in the superpower world. They used human technology all the time.

"Just a little more wine, Whip." Ember cupped his face with her hands. "Give him another piece of pie. He doesn't look so good."

Whip didn't know who she was talking to but pie sounded awfully good. Especially if it was that delicious mudpie.

Somebody took the wine away and put a plate in his hands. Whip glanced down. It was a nice, big piece with shavings of chocolate and... "Is that gold?" he asked.

"Edible. It's our secret ingredient," Christopher Fire said. "I'll tell you what it is if you eat it all."

"Oh. Have no fear. This will soon be an ex-slice of pie." Whip forked the dense chocolaty layers. Something tickled the roof of his mouth.

He felt a little better. He could breathe again.

Mitchell was back, underneath him. Nothing had changed. The sand was still soft, the scent of gold and chocolate wafting between them.

Somebody took the empty plate from his fingers.

"No! I need it!"

Whip was having trouble tearing himself away from the beautiful image of Mitchell beneath him, their hard cocks rubbing against one another. He could hear their moans, feel their passion for one another on that gorgeous, sandy beach. Waves lapped at their feet and asses...it was like something out of *From Here to Eternity*.

He laughed into Mitchell's mouth at the cold tickle of sea foam.

"Fuck me," Mitchell begged, looking up at him. Whip kissed him. He heard an eagle soaring overhead. The dream was so clear, so intense he could hear the flap of the bird's wings beating in time to Mitchell's heart.

He wriggled down to capture Mitchell's cock with his tongue again. He could taste it. Really taste it.

"Whip."

He opened his eyes. Misery washed over him. He couldn't tell anyone what he'd just experienced. He could still taste his lover. He'd sound like a nutcase if he said so.

Christopher was kneeling in front of him now. "Are you okay, Whip?"

Love and concern shone in the gifted chef's eyes. Whip nodded. Hope and hurt warred in his chest. He realised now why they'd given him more pie. He'd related what Mitchell had experienced earlier.

If what he'd seen in his mental darkness was true, then Mitchell had experienced a horrendous childhood. So had Alicia.

"I'm sorry I had to give you a piece of mudpie laced with a love potion." Christopher gazed up at him.

Whip shook his head. "I'm not sorry. I love the movie in my mind. The good one, I mean."

I don't want it to be a dream. I want it to be real.

"I know you do," Christopher said, rubbing Whip's arm. He was bringing Whip back. Back to where he didn't want to be. He wanted to be with Mitchell. On the beach, making love with him.

"How much of that stuff did you give him?" Daine whispered to Christopher.

"A double shot."

"Wow. That's potent." Daine was kneeling beside Christopher now. Whip felt a rush of heat from Christopher's hand on his arm. Unfortunately, the man's touch was bringing him back to earth.

Whip frowned at the men who were urging him away from his mental and emotional paradise.

"When Mitchell gets back here, I want a large mudpie laced to the gills."

"You won't need it." Daine beamed up at him.

"He can have it if he wants," Christopher said. "I promise you, we'll make you that pie. And we'll help you find that beach."

Whip felt a whoosh of affection for the powerful mage.

"So, what do you think of it? It's our latest creation. Better than Valium, right?"

Whip could still feel the sea foam licking at his feet. "Oh, yeah."

"We think it might be a great aphrodisiac. Mudpies in an array of potency. Better than Viagra."

"And the gold leaf on the top?"

"That's the magic."

"I want a whole pie made just of that."

Everybody laughed.

"I can see why," Daine said finally. "It makes you feel wonderful with none of the side effects of a drug. Tell me, can you still feel it?"

"Yeah. I feel the water. It's so nice on my toes." Whip almost giggled. "What the hell is happening to me? I feel so...goofy."

"The potion activates your deepest passions, awakens your romantic fantasy. The sensations it produces drain from your feet, grounding you as you come back to earth, without losing the high completely," Daine said.

"It's fantastic. I'll do some ads for you." Whip gazed down at them. "I'll pay you anything. Can I have another piece?"

Christopher had his hand on Whip's chest. "And his heartbeat is completely normal. The loopy grin...that's a big giveaway. I'm guessing you're really head over heels for Mitchell."

"Yeah." Whip didn't mind admitting it. "This is better than drugs."

He could feel Mitchell's mouth against his. He wanted to return his kisses. Whip slid down in his seat.

"Oh…yeah."

Daine and Christopher caught him, pushing him back. Whip tried to sit up straight. He couldn't remember the guys giving him the first slice of mudpie. One minute they were all holding hands. They could see a vision of Mitchell tied up in a cave somewhere. He had tried to join them in sending telepathic messages to Mitchell. It had worked for a few minutes but the connection had broken.

Somebody had interfered with it. Whip's mind cleared now.

"Friday Otis Doombringer interfered with our connection," he said, remembering.

"It doesn't mean it's bad," Christopher assured him.

"I don't know…" Whip had tuned into Mitchell's mind. He'd seen shocking images of a young Mitchell and Alicia in a car with their mother. As long as he was alive, Whip would never forget the way Mitchell had tried to protect his little sister, the horror of seeing their mother slamming the car into their father.

Voices, new voices, shattered his panicked thoughts. He looked up to see two very handsome men walking into the room.

Whip stood, surprised at how strong and confident he suddenly felt.

I can rule the world!

He nudged Christopher. "That mudpie is the bomb."

Christopher winked at him.

Ember and Copper rushed to greet their new guests.

"Whip has had a vision of where Mitchell is," she said, pointing to him. "He's in the ocean."

The two men stared at him. The more muscular one came over to him.

"Hello, Whip. I've seen some of your fights on YouTube. My name is Ty Anglin and I'm a Water

Marshal. This here is Amadis, he's sort of our squadron leader. He's our...spiritual guru, if you will."

"Nice to meet you both." He extended his hand to Ty, who shook his head.

"I don't want to dilute the messages you're receiving. Amadis is going to hold your hand. I want you to think about that dark place in the ocean where you saw Mitchell in your mind's eye. Go back again."

Whip nodded. He felt Amadis taking hold of his hand with cold, clammy fingers. A sudden chill rippled through him, an unpleasant sensation like brain freeze after eating ice cream too fast. He tried to breathe through the pain.

"You're freaking him out," Ty said. "Relax, Amadis."

Amadis dropped Whip's hand and Whip could breathe again.

"I'll give him a small bite of mudpie," Daine said.

"Oooh, yeah." Whip was thrilled until he saw the minute portion in the middle of a golden plate.

"I did say small," Daine reminded him.

Whip took up the tiny golden fork Ember placed on the dish and finished the mudpie off in two bites. The lovely, golden haze in his brain returned, but, just as he was about to rejoin his lover on the beach, Amadis took his free hand again. The bizarre sensation of stepping into frigid liquid returned and Whip gasped.

Mitchell is freezing to death.

No…it's warm. He's afraid. It's getting dark. He can't see land.

Mitchell! I am coming! I'm here!

"I know exactly where he is," Amadis said, dropping Whip's hand again. "We've only got one man in that part of the world. We need to reach him. Pronto."

Whip collapsed against the throne.

Mitchell had heard him! He could still see him, twisting and turning in the water.

"*Whip!*"

"I'm here," Whip said aloud, coming out of the small, dark dream he had shared with Mitchell.

"We have to get him." He looked at the others.

"Help is already on the way," Ember said. She came to him, extending her hand. "Come, Whip, we've ordered an Inter-House Grand Jury. Neither Damek nor Lashdown are responding to messages. We've issued warrants and Earth Marshals are looking for them now. But we have to hurry. Court will be in session in ten minutes."

He let her drag him along the soft, carpeted floor, though each step away from her amazing gold throne seemed to pull him away from his lovely dream with Mitchell.

I'm going to find that beach when all this is over and I'm going to take him there…

"Why are you dragging your feet?" Ember asked, frowning at him.

"I don't want to leave him."

"Foolish child. You're not leaving him. He's right in here." She tapped his chest. Whip bent his head. He didn't want her to see him upset. They were all trying to help him. They were trying to help Mitchell. But what he'd just glimpsed in his mind's eye made him sick to his stomach.

* * * *

Mitchell alternately dog-paddled and trod water, thankful for an ability to swim thanks to several summers spent as a camp counsellor in Long Island. As a kid he'd never been a participant but he'd longed to be there.

At the age of fourteen his mom had relented and let him go.

As a junior counsellor.

She'd held back that particular piece of information until she'd dumped him at the gates of the Rocky Point Recreational Center. Most of the other kids had hated the damned place. Mitchell had loved it, but he should have smelt a rat from the start when she'd asked him if he wanted to go. Luckily for him, she'd picked a surf camp that gave him a respite from her. She'd always seemed to hate Mitchell but with Alicia in a wheelchair his mom was gentler with her than she had been when his sister could walk. He had been unafraid of leaving Alicia with their mother. He'd basked in his independence and slept well, even though the other kids had bitched and moaned about the camp beds and sea-dampened blankets.

Then, the ocean had become his refuge...but this? This was hell. He was tired but knew he had to keep kicking.

The weirdest images kept floating into his mind. He was sitting on a beach with Whip. A beach? Where? He longed for the touch of sand...of hard ground beneath his body. Whip kissing him...touching him... The dream seduced him, relaxed his mind.

He shook the lusty images from his head. He'd heard that people near death saw their lives flashing before them. It hadn't happened to him when his mother had almost killed him in that car. Now that he was probably close to death again, all he could see, feel, think about...taste...was Whip.

Would Whip laugh if he knew?

Keep paddling.

He turned over on his back, staring up at the sky as he bobbed around like a drunken cork. He had to give his back, shoulders, arms and legs a break. He used his hands to stay afloat—just his hands, like lazy flippers. He could hear the sound of the ocean. A bird soared overhead.

Mitchell jerked himself up. A bird was a sign of land, wasn't it? Or maybe a vessel? He tried to look as far ahead as he could, twisting around slowly. What time was it? What day? How much time had he lost?

Was Foti really a monster, like his mother?

He moved in a second slow circle, trying to get his bearings. He'd lost not only his sense of time but that of direction as well. He picked out the bird's white underbelly as it careened across the sky.

Follow it, idiot.

He began to stroke, breaststroke, so he could keep his gaze on the bird. In the distance he could see a vessel. A ship. Maybe it was some kind of fishing trawler. The bird would be attracted to fish.

Keep paddling. Ignore the burning in your legs. Just swim. Imagine it's Whip and Alicia on that ship. Waiting for you.

He began to swim freestyle now, to speed up the process, but he was so exhausted he didn't seem to get very far. He was no closer to the ship...or else it was moving farther away from him. He was so wiped out he kept swallowing water. He couldn't turn his head out of the water enough to breathe in air.

This is futile. I gotta breaststroke. I gotta take my time. I gotta get there.

He'd seen the movie *Open Water* and it had seemed to him at the time that a ghastly mistake such as being left at sea during a scuba dive would be horrendous.

"Why am I thinking about that?" he said aloud. Hearing his own voice helped bolster his spirits so he kept talking.

"Tell yourself a story," he muttered. He lay on his back for a moment staring up at the sky again. He gulped deep breaths, each one increasingly painful. He fought off the weird urge to just let go...to just let himself drop beneath the surface of the waves.

"Stop. Tell a story. What were the stories you used to tell the kids in camp? *Moby Dick*. That's a good story. Um...how does it go again?"

He hummed to himself. "I think Jonah—is that his name?—is sitting in the whale's mouth selling oranges to the tourists."

Wait...that's not right. Are there tourists in that book? I don't think so. Maybe I didn't read it. What did I read?

His body felt like a stone when he resumed swimming, the breaststroke slowly carrying him towards the ship that was now even farther away. He wouldn't call out. He'd conserve his strength.

The Hardy Boys. Yeah...I loved me some Hardy Boys.

He began to sing. "*Ging gang gooly gooly wash wash ging gang goo. Ging gang goo.* What is that? An Australian song. A senior camp counsellor taught me that song. And then...later that night he sucked my cock. Yep. I discovered I was gay. It took me a long time to ever trust a man again.

"And let that be a warning to you, children. When a camp counsellor invites you into his cabin late at night, chances are good he doesn't want to discuss your surfing abilities."

He bobbed around a bit. Talking distracted him from the freakin' agony in his arms as he swam.

Keep talking.

"Where was I? Oh, yes. That movie—you know...*Open Water*... That scared me. And now it's happening to me!" He let out a bark of hysterical laughter.

This can't be happening to me.

But it is...

Focus on a story. What did you tell the kids?

"Didn't I tell them a story already?"

My mind is playing tricks on me. Isn't that what happens when you die at sea? I know I've read about it. First you become dehydrated. And fuck, I am thirsty. So thirsty. And my stomach aches. Is that normal? I need an orange. Or did I sell them all to the tourists?

And then you become disorientated. Yeah. I am that... And in the end you succumb to drowning, or you get eaten by sharks.

Yummy!

"Which would be worse?" he asked aloud. "Drowning or getting eaten?"

He found himself surprisingly picking up speed.

"I can swim! I'll reach that boat. And then I want a nice cup of tea."

A cup of tea? Is that what I want?

Yeah. I want to feel warm again.

He was certain he was closer now. He could see the waves slapping against the hill of the ship.

But straight ahead of him now was...

A shark.

Heading right for him.

He thought about sinking...just letting himself drop. But it was no use. The shark picked up speed. He let out a ragged sob as the shark stopped an inch from his face. Only it wasn't a shark.

Hell...it looks like a man wearing a shark fin suit!

"Mitchell, you don't know me," the man said, "but I am from the Water House. My name is Vincent Garrison. And I am a shark."

Chapter Ten

It's happened. I'm disorientated and flipping out. Sharks don't talk.

Except...this shark was a man. And he was wearing a shark suit.

"Don't be afraid," the shark man said. "I won't bite." He turned and waved to the vessel, giving an ear-piercing whistle.

Vincent Garrison grabbed Mitchell and turned him around, holding him by his upper body as he stroked. It felt so nice to have somebody else do the hard work. Mitchell closed his eyes, unable to stay awake anymore.

Then he heard voices. Oh, they were so loud and people were grabbing him.

He felt himself rising from the water. He spilled onto a deck. Somebody turned him over. Water streamed out of his mouth.

Towels covered him and he was up again. Unable to stand unaided, he allowed the shark man to put him into a chair on the deck. He gulped at the bottle of cold water somebody else gave him. It felt so good.

"Mitchell?" The man leant down to him. "My name is Finn Garrison. Your lover, Whip Jackson, is on the phone. He's frantic with worry."

"He is?" Mitchell took the gigantic piece of equipment he recognised as a satellite phone and put it to his ear. My, but it felt good to hear Whip's voice again, even if he was screaming at Mitchell.

"Say something!" Whip hollered.

"I think I sold all my oranges."

"You...what?"

Finn Garrison snatched the phone out of his hand.

"He's disoriented. His hands and head...there are some deep cuts. God knows how he survived. We're gonna take him to the hospital."

Mitchell gazed up at Finn. He didn't have a shark fin. But the man beside him did.

"It's okay," the shark man said.

"Where am I?" Mitchell struggled to take it all in.

"You're in the middle of the Bermuda Triangle, son."

* * * *

Whip was able to concentrate a little better on the boarding process for the bullet train to Mexico knowing that Mitchell was okay. What the hell oranges had he been talking about? He shook his head and followed the others into the carriage. He'd never been to the revered Earth Court in the holy city of Teotihuacán, Mexico. He'd heard about it, but like so many other things in the realm of Elementals, he'd thought it was a myth.

He hardly felt the pull and whoosh of the bullet as it soared underground towards the fallen Aztec city. Listed as a World Heritage Site, it tickled him that the most visited archaeological site in Mexico was also the secret meeting place of the Earth people where they settled their legal disputes.

Whip listened when Marcel Paradis stood in front, facing them all. He became his formal self. A glance at Christopher in the semi-darkness showed him gazing adoringly up at his life partner. Marcel in his business mode was impressive, fearsome. His off-work grumpiness, Whip realised, was a front. Marcel was the type preoccupied by worldly matters. He cared about what was right and fixing things that weren't.

As he outlined the pre-trial motions he would present to the Pyramid Chamber of Power, the others listened. All except Njáll. The troll king snored loudly, his head on Alicia's lap. She was nodding off, though trying hard to stay awake.

Sleepiness overcame Whip, too.

What the hell is going on? He started to yawn. The others followed suit.

"Fight it!" Marcel barked. "We're coming closer to the power source and it can be draining. We need to fight it. We need to show our collective strength."

The only ones not nodding off were Ember and Copper Hephaestos. They sat listening to Marcel, bright-eyed and attentive.

Whip fought the crushing indolence that swept over him. Seconds later, he felt much better and caught Ember's winning smile.

"The first judge we need to appeal to, the one we need to convince of superpower tampering, is the High Court Earth Judge, Clay Tillman," Marcel said. "I'm going to defer to Ember and Copper on this since they play pétanque with him."

All eyes turned to Copper, who looked a little embarrassed. "If you think it will help, most certainly we can lead the charge."

He took his wife's hand and kissed it. Whip marvelled at the pair. They looked so young and so in love in spite of their advanced years. Whip studied Copper for a moment. How was it that he had been able to give Alicia her ability to walk back? Well, he and Ember had. Their love had fused into an amazing life force...but how was it that Copper had remained lame?

As the bullet train came to a stop, Whip smelt deep earth. The aroma was nothing like the earth scents in the city. It was rich, strong, sweet and...pure. Yes. It was clean dirt. It was kind of a turn-on.

They spilled out onto a platform of hard-packed earth. Though it was dark and they appeared to be underground, there was a stream of silver light coming from somewhere.

"Oh, the satyrs are here!" Ember gushed, moving towards the sound of stampeding hooves.

"My, they're so handsome!" Alicia seconded.

"No, they're not," grumbled Njáll who was standing right beside Whip.

All conversation stopped and everyone turned to stare at Whip. They obviously thought he was the one who'd made the comment but Whip knew better than to disparage the highly vain goat-like creatures who were mainstays of the Earth House's elemental force.

"You're no oil painting either, sunshine," the leader said to Whip. As the others followed him, Whip's spirits sank. They each had been conjured horses to ride. Not just horses, magnificent black steeds.

He was given a pane. Whip had experienced run-ins with this prickly tribe of nature spirits. They had the heads and torsos of men, but their faces were goat-like. They had the horns, bodies, legs and tails of goats.

And personalities to match.

Whip thanked the pane assigned to him. The creature looked less than thrilled and Whip found it difficult to mount it. If he didn't know any better he'd swear it was trying to toss him off each time he got his leg over the creature's hairy back.

Finally he made it and Whip did his best to ignore the amused grins on his companions' faces. He rode the pane up the steep incline towards the earth's surface. He was astonished to find they had arrived right outside the ancient pyramids of Teotihuacán.

Silence, save for the rhythmic clop of hooves accompanied their journey.

"This is the Avenue of the Dead," Whip heard Njáll tell Alicia. "People still come here to honour their ancestors."

Whip could see no civvies around, but certainly felt the profound power of the ancient city said to have been wondrous in its living form, breathtaking still even in ruins.

Three huge pyramids—one, he knew, represented the moon, another the sun—stood in what was supposed to be a geometrically symbolic outline.

"No wonder they call it the birthplace of the gods," Whip said.

The pane he road tossed him an odd look over his shoulder. Whip's ride was less than comfortable but he was afraid of upsetting the creature and held on a little tighter with his thighs. He caught Njáll's chagrined smile but chose to ignore it. At the next wrestling meeting, he'd suggest that they should revive the noble art of dwarf tossing.

Whip and the others took in the incredible sight of some of the oldest pyramids in the world. The city's origin was still debated, but it was generally accepted that it dated back to pre-Colombian times, somewhere between a hundred years to five hundred after the death of Christ.

It was no secret that the pyramids and the surrounding platforms must have held great significance and power to ancient tribes of Aztecs and allegedly even Mayans. Much of the city had been burned centuries ago during the eruption of the Xitle Volcano and later due to internal battles. These battles ultimately destroyed what was supposed to have been a utopian existence — taking with it the keys and clues to the site's most profound secrets.

Whip vowed to study more about the place...but for now his small group stopped outside one particularly tall pyramid.

"Ah," Justice Paradis said. "Here we are. The Pyramid of the Sun."

The view from here of lush grounds, well-tended trees and the remnants of ancient buildings was alluring, but they had business to attend to.

An invisible door in the pyramid opened and the horses all whinnied. Everybody climbed off the animals' backs.

"Thank you, Jorge," Ember called after her steed.

Whip got tossed on his ass by the pane. Still, he thanked the creature, who spat, "Whatever, asshole," and galloped away.

It hadn't been Whip's fault that he'd once conducted an online romance with a man, fallen in love with his face only to discover his real identity when they met for coffee. Evidently the pane community had long memories and still took his rejection hard.

Inside the pyramid, in sharp contrast with the outside world, was a hive of activity. Men and women scurried up and down stone stairs built into the sides of the slanted walls. A glass-walled elevator appeared out of nowhere.

A door opened with a resounding ping and a female troll in a brown suit grinned up at them.

"Going down, Commander Jørgensen?" she asked.

"Cornelia!" Njáll rushed towards her and they exchanged an emotional embrace. Whip saw the jealous expression on Alicia's face.

"Alicia," Njáll said, turning to her. "I want you to meet my sister. Cornelia, I want you to meet my fiancée, Alicia Dykins."

Cornelia glanced up and down Alicia as if finding her wanting.

She said nothing, ignoring Alicia's extended hand.

"We're in a hurry," Marcel said. They all climbed into the elevator. Whip's head swivelled in all directions taking in the constant stream of foot traffic on the stairs. Doors opened and closed along the walls, and inside the elevator Cornelia muttered darkly, "Mother won't like this at all."

"Our mother's dead," Njáll said as they got out of the elevator.

"She still won't like it," Cornelia said and closed the door in his face. Ember led the way along a narrow corridor. Njáll kept trying to comfort a stricken Alicia.

"My sister's a loon. Look where she works, for lord's sake! She could live on a perfectly good dung heap, but look where she's chosen!"

"A dung heap?" Alicia glanced down at him. "What d'you mean a dung heap?"

Whip didn't hear the rest of the conversation. They'd been whisked into what looked like the interior of an adobe-style building. Mud walls, a dome-shaped roof and courtroom chairs made of sandstone.

They hurried to the front rows where a bailiff in a similar brown uniform to Cornelia's held a stone tablet in his hand.

"The court will now hear the petition from—" He gaped at the stone. "This is unusual—an emergency petition regarding the violation of superpower Earth Powers and an interlocutory judgement."

He beckoned the near-empty room and Whip's party surged forwards.

"We're here to see Judge Tillman," Marcel announced, violating his own suggestion that Ember and Copper lead the charge.

"And you are?" The bailiff gave him a baleful once-over similar to the one Cornelia had subjected poor Alicia to.

"Justice Marcel Paradis of the Imperial Fire House Court. May we please see him now?"

"How...?" The bailiff looked confused as he took in the motley crew assembled in front of him. "Why...?"

He scratched his chin but did nothing.

Seconds later, a door opened and a massive man stepped into the courtroom. He must have been seven feet tall. No...more. A giant. *Wow.* He was handsome, too.

The giant caught Whip's gaze and grinned.

"Good afternoon, Marcel, I see you've brought company." The giant's voice rumbled deep, like the earth itself. It was so sexy it made Whip want to get naked and roll all over in a field of daisies.

"Welcome all. Please sit. And keep it brief. I made an exception for your emergency petition but I've got a full slate today." The judge sat in his seat, uniformed trolls on either side of him.

Marcel turned to Ember and Copper. Not missing their cue, the couple stepped forwards.

Ember turned to her husband, who began to talk.

"Your honour, we are here united—"

There was the sound of doors opening and voices yelling. Everyone present turned to see the new arrivals.

Though he'd never seen Ember and Copper's offspring, there could be no question the handsome, flame-haired men and the elegant, Titian-haired woman were their children. Accompanying them were various attorneys from the fabled superpowers' law firm of Arden, Bainbridge, Chinook and Damek. Everyone, of course, except Damek.

"Sorry it took so long, Justice Tillman," a red-faced man said, addressing the judge. "I am Ignatius Arden, the Fire House attorney. Chinook and Bainbridge are with me. They represent Air and Water."

"I know who you are," the giant said, sounding cross. "You're late."

"Sorry, your honour. We had a hard time with our transportation. Seems the panes have gone on strike." He shot Whip a withering look.

"Get on with it."

Ember, who'd been busy hugging her children, spoke.

"As you know, your eminence, this matter concerns Mr. Mitchell Dykins, who until several days ago had no idea that he had any superpowers. He's a young man whose circumstances in life have been difficult, at best."

"I am aware of his story and I agree. He's an exemplary young man and an asset to the House of Earth." The judge finally smiled. "As is his sister."

"Well, your honour, my husband and I have come to know both of them only today and their hearts are pure. We have given Alicia the ability to walk — an ability, I might add, that was taken away by her mother, who was once a bailiff here."

The judge nodded.

This was news to Whip. He'd had no idea that Kathy Dykins had been part of the superpower realm.

"She dabbled in undesirable powers and we evicted her," Tillman said. "At least, my predecessor did, which in my opinion was a grave mistake. She had tremendous potential, but outcast into the civilian world she had no defence against dark forces. She had no willpower or self-control."

He picked up a file and glanced through it.

"And now, it seems, she has found immortality."

"No," Copper said, "She is an entity able to hide in shadows. She has taken over the mind — finally, after years of effort — of her brother, Friday Otis Doombringer. She has been residing in a particularly...virulent Mongolian death worm, and more recently, the alter ego of Whip 'Mudshark' Jackson."

Whip froze. *My God...she's the reason my pit personality turned!*

"We believe she is very dangerous. We believe she infiltrated the minds of Goyathlay Damek and Early Lashdown, neither of whom has been seen in recent days. And both have ignored their official summons."

Tillman nodded. "I have no doubt this is true, but we can forget about hunting down Mr. Damek. He's here. As a matter of fact, he's in my private chambers with Mitchell Dykins."

Mitchell's here! Whip's whole body vibrated with happiness. *He's here... God...I hope he's okay.*

"Mr. Jackson," the judge said, surprising him by calling out to him. "I want you to take the witness stand and tell me what you saw in the vision enhanced for you by Ember Hephaestos."

"Gladly, your honour." He took his seat in the famous limestone chair he'd heard about. A weird shiver ran through him. He knew he wouldn't have to bother taking an oath. The witness chair coaxed the truth out of you.

He described meeting Mitchell. He described the earthquakes, their sudden drop into the mudpit in New York and how Mitchell had beaten him. He told the court all about how he'd fallen for Mitchell and, he hoped, how Mitchell had for him, but how frustrated he was that he'd been unable to protect him from his mother.

"I have no experience of possession...of demonic forces. Although I am involved in the superpower world, most people I meet are honest. I am more afraid of civvies than Elementals because...well...we all know what it means to violate our powers." He took a deep breath. "We know we have to practice our elemental superpowers for good, not evil. I've never experienced anything as evil as the dark heart of Kathy Dykins."

Whip glanced at Alicia. "It grieves me terribly that you and your brother had the lives you did. But I'm here now. We're all here. And we love you."

Alicia burst into tears.

Even the judge broke down. And the sight of a giant sobbing wasn't pretty. They had to evacuate the courtroom to let it dry out.

In a private room, as they waited, Copper limped over to Whip and put a hand on his shoulder. "Now you know why I gladly allowed the gods to force me to keep my limp. It's nothing to me. But the power to love, to help people like Alicia and Mitchell... I would willingly give both my arms and my legs to help them."

And Whip finally understood.

A bailiff brought them pizza and lasagne. Whip was starving, and so, apparently, were the others.

"Earthy, solid food," Ember said, approvingly.

Whip adored her. He was sure she ate more lavishly at home, but maybe not. She seemed so down to earth...and real. He longed to see Mitchell but said nothing. He had to let the legal process run its course.

Back in the courtroom a few minutes later, Copper raised the issue of Mitchell's last fight, the one a possessed Lashdown had forced him into.

"Glauconite-enhanced mud was used in an effort to kill the opponent. As you know, traces of it were found in Doombringer's last fight before he went missing," Copper said.

He paused, as if weighing his words. "I know that many in the superpower community think that glauconite is a bit like the supernatural date drug because it can produce a high, but it's a very sinister poison."

The judge nodded. "Yes, I know."

"We should have revealed the truth sooner. Glauconite taken in large quantities raises the dead. It can because in its pure form it involves the cells of dead animals, and can actually be used to conjure dead beasts from long ago. It's long been my suspicion that Kathy Dykins was able to raise her own Mongolian death worm, a creature many centuries extinct. She raised it, finally inhabiting it. The worm has turned, as the saying goes. It is a creature simply bred to kill."

There was a collective gasp in the courtroom.

"I believe it was a severe error of judgement for the Earth House judge to keep all of this information secret. It's obvious that somebody knew that Kathy Dykins had found a way for her spirit to return to Earth upon her death in order to seek and destroy her brother and her children. The same children she took her deep, soul rage out upon when she was forced to abandon our world.

"Friday Otis loves Mitchell and Alicia and resisted his sister's power for two years, but his mind has finally broken. I would like to petition the court that when we find him, we cure him of his possession, and of course, Justice Lashdown, too. I'm afraid I also don't trust Damek and suggest, respectfully, that he be submitted for elemental superpower cleansing as well."

Tillman studied him. "Fair enough. I accept all these suggestions. There's just one problem, though."

"What's that?"

"We need to apprehend Kathy Dykins and her brother. They have sent a message to Damek saying they want to schedule a wrestling match."

A murmur of dismay went up in the courtroom, but Tillman held up his hand.

"He has been very transparent in his dealings with the court since he came here under guard of the Water Marshals. He has not revealed to Kathy and Friday that we have ordered an emergency court hearing. And it will stay that way.

"Until further notice, you are all to remain here. All communication with the outside world until we can set up this wrestling match is forbidden."

He gave every single person in the room a hard stare. "Is this clearly understood?"

"Yes, your honour," they said as one.

He titled his head. "I can't hear you. Is that understood?"

"Yes, your honour!"

He grinned. "I confess, I heard you the first time, but I never get sick of it!" As the bailiff collected everybody's cell phones, he smiled at Whip. "As for you, young man, there is somebody in my private chambers who I believe is most anxious to see you."

Whip was on his feet in an instant. His companions patted his shoulders and back as he moved past them. He held his breath as he followed the trolls and there…

There, sitting in a chair in a dark room, but now springing to action and mercifully into his arms, was Mitchell.

"Thank God," Whip said, his mouth against his lover's.

For several minutes the two men kissed. Whip thought they'd both stop breathing if they didn't take a break.

"I want you to fuck me, and I want a cup of tea," Mitchell said. "In that order."

Mitchell was disappointed when Whip stepped back and released him. "Are you okay?"

"I'm fine. But I hope I'm going to be even better in a moment."

Whip's eyes narrowed. "You are gonna get fucked and you will never forget it. Give me your hand back. That's mine." Whip slipped it back into his warm grip and their eyes connected.

His lover's hips thrust towards Mitchell but Mitchell knew it was involuntary. They were so into each other, their cocks gravitated towards one another.

Mitchell averted his gaze for a moment. He had to make Whip wait until he could explain everything.

"I think my family may be insane. My mother—"

"I don't give a fuck about her."

"But she's a killer. I—"

"It can wait. What can't wait is handling your first necessity, then the second." Whip smiled at him.

He cocked his head and dragged Mitchell away from the judge's chambers. Mitchell was surprised when they stepped into what appeared to be a pathway inside a lush, dense rain forest. They traversed a thicket of tropical trees. Mitchell held Whip's hand tighter on instinct. He didn't want to lose him a second time.

"I have no idea where we are but this is beautiful," Whip said, glancing at him. "Do you suppose the judge conceived this precious place to give us some privacy?"

"It wouldn't surprise me." The judge had been so kind—beyond kind to Mitchell, actually—and he felt safe as they pressed into a fallen canopy of soft green grass and…oddly…daisies.

They were breathing hard, both from the exercise and from each other. *Damn it.* Mitchell needed to kiss him. They fell into each other once more. Mitchell moved his mouth over his face and throat and down to his nipples. He loved how Whip squirmed every place he licked him, loved the salty taste to his skin as he peeled off his clothes. Whip was so hard now. Mitchell couldn't believe he could get his Adonis that hard just kissing him.

"Oh, yeah…and it never happened before. I see your face and I get hard." Whip was reading his thoughts again.

Mitchell had been afraid their budding, tenuous connection might have been severed.

"That makes two of us then." His smile widened when his hand touched the bulge lurking against his belly.

"Hurry," he whispered as the wind picked up. He was afraid they'd have to go back and that was the last thing Mitchell wanted. He held Whip in his arms. They kissed, grabbing one another's faces and asses, fingers straying to one another's cocks, assuring themselves of hard evidence.

Whip pushed him to the ground. He lay on his back receiving Whip's hard body between his parted thighs. One look from Whip and Mitchell drew his knees up, Whip dropping kisses on them both before dipping down and plunging his face to Mitchell's ass. Mitchell bucked at the new contact with Whip's hot tongue.

He quickly lifted his face again. "Stroke your cock for me," he commanded Mitchell whose body jerked underneath him.

He held his breath when Whip's tongue stabbed at his ass, then flicked up to his balls. Mitchell's mouth dropped open and he looked up at Whip with a burnished gaze. Whip lifted his face again then went right back to work, licking his ass, using his thumb to rub circles on his hole, gently sticking it into Mitchell.

Mitchell began stroking his cock now that he could move again. Pleasure had paralysed him.

"Oh...no... Let me... I'll do that." Whip hunched up, his mouth devouring Mitchell's cock.

Mitchell let out a shout of joy but then Whip took his mouth off him, releasing the now-purple head with a pop.

Whip reached under Mitchell, slapped his ass lightly and sucked Mitchell into his mouth again, making him cry out. His hand moved slowly up and down Mitchell's cock, his tongue chasing his fingertips. He took his tongue away, still keeping Mitchell's ass in his hot hands.

He returned to Mitchell's cock, licking only the tip of the head. The only sounds in the universe were of one man voraciously licking another and the sound of Mitchell begging, "Please…" Whip plunged his mouth over Mitchell's cock and sucked it into his throat. He wrestled Mitchell on the ground, and Mitchell ground against Whip's fingers, which moved in maddening circles over his asshole.

Whip sucked Mitchell's cock until he came. Whip waited until the eruption abated before mounting him, burying his cock in Mitchell's burning ass.

Mitchell felt as if the rainforest—the skies, the soft rain that fell, the sounds of leaves rustling—all joined in their pleasure. Mitchell felt Whip's wild pounding, his shouted words of love and tears leaked from his eyes.

"I love you too," he said as Whip came deep inside him.

For long moments afterwards Whip lay on top of him before slowly withdrawing from Mitchell's ass. They lay, legs akimbo, on the forest floor for what seemed like a long time. Mitchell couldn't keep the grin from his face as Whip raised himself on one elbow, looking down into his face.

"That was great!"

"Yeah." Whip nodded, kissing him. Things soon turned serious, their hard cocks straining at one another as Mitchell held both cocks in his hands.

"Ahem," said a female voice from somewhere deep in the forest. "Knock knock."

"Who's there?" Whip asked, winking down at Mitchell.

"It's me, Alicia."

"Alicia who?"

"Alicia Keys, funny man. You know which Alicia. I want to see my brother. Are you decent?"

"Not yet," Mitchell said as Whip got off him. So much for afterglow. They hopped around, looking for their discarded clothing, and redressed.

"What the hell are you wearing?" Whip suddenly asked.

"Oh...Ty Anglin lent me some of his things."

"Did he now?"

Mitchell liked the mad-jealous expression on Whip's face.

"Are you decent?" Alicia asked again. She sounded exasperated.

"Yes," Mitchell said, zipping up the fly of the ill-fitting bell-bottom jeans Ty had lent him. He did think the man could have lent him something from this millennium but beggars couldn't be choosy.

"What do you think?" Alicia asked, stepping forwards, a tea tray in hand.

Mitchell gasped. Tears sprang into his eyes. "Darling girl," he said.

Thankfully, Whip rushed over and grabbed the tray before Mitchell upended it as he grabbed his sister in a hug. He twirled her around, so happy to hear her laughter. He set her down when she claimed dizziness.

They sat on the grass, all three of them, drinking tea and enjoying bite-size blackberry shortbread cupcakes.

"These are incredible," Mitchell said. "I've never tasted anything like them."

"They are Justice Tillman's favourites," Alicia said.

"Wait until you try the mudpie." Whip poured Mitchell more tea. "I've ordered us a whole one."

"I love mudpie," Mitchell said. Alicia and Whip told him about Ember and Copper. He told them about being rescued at sea by the shark man.

"It turns out I hallucinated a lot of things but not him. He's the coolest old dude I've ever met."

They were interrupted by the bailiff ordering them to the courtroom.

"We're back in session," he said, clicking his fingers. Their lush rainforest idyll vanished and they were back in the judge's chambers.

"I think I love this place," Alicia said, taking Mitchell's hand. The three of them walked into the courtroom, Whip putting a protective arm around Mitchell. His long reach held Alicia, too.

"Mr. Damek has been hospitalised and will remain here until further notice," the judge said. "We are still unable to locate Justice Lashdown but"—he gave a disgusted sneer—"according to his Twitter account, he is in New Zealand at a Lady Gaga concert. So either his account's been hacked or he's playing us for fools."

The judge glowered. It was a frightening sight.

Tillman took a moment to compose himself. "We've taken control of Damek's cell phone under the authority of the court. He has been conducting conversations with a woman named Lucy who works at World Wide Wrestlers, Inc. We believe Kathy Dykins and her brother are in New York now at the offices. We suspect Kathy has taken possession of Lucy and no doubt will be contacting Whip Jackson and Mitchell Dykins asking them to participate in a charitable mudpit match.

"However, we believe there is no charity to which the fans' ticket money has been allocated. We believe this is a death match."

The judge was interrupted by the shrill ring of a cell phone. He picked it up and stared at the screen.

"Mr. Jackson, I believe this is Lucy calling you now to schedule your bout. You are to agree to everything without giving her any information. If she asks, Damek is fine. Understood?"

Whip left his seat and raced over to the bench. The judge leant down and handed him his phone.

Mitchell heard his lover's terse words followed by his rushed assurances. "Oh, Damek's fine... He's having drinks by the pool. See you in New York."

He ended the call and looked up at Tillman.

"How did I do?"

"Fine, Mr. Jackson. Now let's discuss how to keep you two alive and get Kathy, Lashdown and Friday into protective custody."

He gazed down the bench, pointing at Chinook, the Air Court attorney.

"Mr. Chinook, please arrange for the swiftest air transportation to New York. I dislike bullet trains. They make my bum ache."

Chapter Eleven

Mitchell was nervous. He paced the hotel room, expecting something to go wrong, some disaster to strike before they could get into the ring underground at Madison Square Garden. He was wearing his fighting trunks and boots and had a robe over them, but he couldn't seem to get back the primal confidence he'd felt the last time he'd stepped into his ringwear.

The centaur that had volunteered for the event galloped across the room and Mitchell worried he'd muck up the place and that security would chuck them all out. They'd already had the front desk personnel calling three times saying the neighbours were complaining of horses whinnying and dogs barking.

It had taken some effort not to say, *'They're not dogs — it's a cerberus, a three-headed dog sent to protect me and Whip.'*

And the horse…well…he was a unicorn and feeling a bit fussy because room service had neglected to send up his cornflakes.

Mitchell had assured the desk staff that there were no dogs or horses in the room. But the single cerberus was a nightmare. The three-headed beast might have been of the superpower realm but each of the three heads had its own gnarly disposition. Then again, it did guard the gates of Hades.

And the three heads acted like demon dogs, too...to everyone except Alicia and Ember.

The two women in the group were very excited about the mud fight. Alicia would be mistress of ceremonies and Ember, who'd apparently harboured a secret passion to see a live mud fight for years, had bought opera glasses from a little antique shop in Soho. She'd even bought a stunning new floor-length dress made of an antique gold and amber Banerasi sari woven with modern cerise-coloured silk. She looked gorgeous.

She and Copper had ringside seats. Mitchell worried that her fantasies would all be for naught when she found herself splattered in mud. Their children were working security detail along with several other volunteers.

Tickets for the show had sold out within hours and Mitchell knew that, for the hefty, bumped-up prices, the fans expected to see a show. Mitchell and Whip would give them one, but not the kind his mother and uncle expected. Before anyone would be killed, Marshals from each of the realms would descend upon the pit and arrest Kathy and Friday should they appear in the mud.

As for their opponents...all Mitchell knew was that he and Whip were supposed to be up against two unknown fighters.

"Expect a trick," Justice Tillman had warned. "Your mother's getting worried because she's been contacting Damek in code and we haven't been able to decipher the text messages yet."

"Show me," Mitchell said.

He studied his mother's most recent text and frowned.

"That's weird."

"It sure is, isn't it?" The judge shrugged.

"No, I mean this is a language my mom made up when we were kids. How would Damek know it?"

Tillman stared at him. "Well, she has him bedazzled so he understands it. What does she say?"

Mitchell felt Whip's arm around him as Mitchell took a deep breath.

"She says, 'Show no mercy—kill both of them.'" He glanced at Whip. "I guess that means us."

Whip shook his head. "Let her try."

The room phone rang again and he picked up the receiver. After a brief exchange he said, "We should go. That was the front desk staff again. Security is coming."

Whip turned towards the cerberus. "Pookie, stop chewing the curtains. There's a good boy...er...boys...er... Come on, the portal's in the bathroom."

Marcel and Christopher, Daine and Phillip, Ember and Copper joined Whip and Mitchell in the bathroom watching Alicia, Justice Tillman and the superpower animals disappearing down a dark corridor directly behind the toilet.

Njáll was sulking. Ever since his revelation about his fondness for dung, things had cooled between him and Alicia and he was in a sour mood.

"Are you coming?" Mitchell asked him.

"'Course I am," Njáll said. "Wouldn't miss it for anything."

He pushed his way ahead of them. Mitchell and Whip went in next, followed by the others. Whip took Mitchell's hand as they began to descend deeper. Mitchell could hear the crowd roaring now. It lifted his spirits, stirred something deep within him.

Mitchell feared this part of himself because he hated to cause pain.

"What is it? What's wrong?" Whip asked, sensing his anxiety immediately.

"Whip… What if…what if I'm like her?"

"You're not a monster. Neither is she. Well…at least she wasn't. She dabbled in black magic and lost her way, but you're not her. You are a good man. And we're going to fight her. We're going to win."

"But I read her file. She did terrible things. She put curses on people. My father…he was married to her best friend who died under suspicious circumstances. I can't believe she wasn't put in jail. She married my dad but it was a terrible marriage. They never stopped fighting. I—"

"Black magic came between them, Mitch," Whip said. "The dark arts can never prosper. Because she had children, she was given a second chance at a different life. All her powers were stripped of her. She had the man she said she wanted. It should have been enough. It should have been *plenty*."

Mitchell knew this. Justice Tillman had explained it all, saying his mother had slipped through the cracks in the superpower legal system.

"We should have been keeping a closer eye on her," he'd told Mitchell during their private discussion in his chambers. "We had no idea her evil pursuits continued. I would never have authorised her release into society unless I'd known she was cured from her shadows."

Instead, Kathy Dykins had tormented the three people she was supposed to love. At least he and Alicia had survived. They had each other. He glanced over his shoulder at his new friends who'd shown such amazing support.

Out of the darkness, Bixby, Mitchell's fluffer from the last fight, suddenly appeared. He made Mitchell jump.

"I'm here to help you, sir," he said. Mitchell peered down at the little man in the darkness.

"He told me you have sex with your fluffer, is that true?" Mitchell asked Whip. Even in the bad light Mitchell could see his lover was embarrassed.

"We fooled around once...a long time ago before I met you." At Mitchell's incredulous stare he said, "I was drunk. They gave me dwarf wine!" He stared accusingly at Bixby, who was rolling around the narrow pathway, laughing.

"We need to hurry," Marcel reminded them. They all stepped over Bixby.

"And I'll fluff my man's privates myself, thanks!" Whip shouted over his shoulder. He seemed pissed as he gripped Mitchell's hand and yanked him to the right.

"See you later," he told the others.

Mitchell glimpsed Daine and Phillip's worried expressions. There was no time for goodbyes or thanks... No time for thought. The next thing Mitchell knew, he was on his way to the arena. Unseen hands removed the robes from his shoulders and from Whip's, too. Whip looked at him.

"Don't believe anything you see," he said, "I know she will try to separate us and make you believe I want to hurt you. When all this is over, I promise you a lifetime of beaches and mudpies."

The crowd's roars reached a deafening pitch.

"Believe me when I tell you that I love you. Listen to me in the ring. Listen to the voice in your head. I know it's noisy...but you have to trust me. She can't violate our trust. She has no idea we communicate that way. Ignore the fans... Ignore the insanity. Just listen only to me."

"Okay," Mitchell said. Whip kissed his cheek and plunged ahead, entering the ring first, leaving Mitchell in the wings with his own crewmembers who were rushing around him. Bixby and two helpers were trying to oil his body.

Mitchell wanted to shoo them away like flies. He was nervous and worried. He had never seen so many people in one place in his life. What if it all went wrong?

Huge screens mounted around the arena showed Whip striding into the ring. He had his arms raised in triumph, the conquering hero. There was no hint of the worry Mitchell had seen on his lover's features just a few moments ago.

He stared at the images of a gigantic mudpit that seemed to be alive. It spat mud and each time it did, the crowd reacted with *oohs* and *aahs*.

"It's been treated with heat to counteract any attempts Kathy might make to infuse it with glauconite," Justice Tillman suddenly said, appearing beside him. "I should warn you it is perfectly safe and nothing she does can counteract it. It does, however, have some side effects."

Mitchell could hardly think. He glanced up once more at the screens as the crowd went mad. Alicia and the centaur were in the ring.

"What side effects?" Mitchell asked.

"It makes you feel terribly itchy," the judge said as Bixby slapped his butt.

"You're up, toots!"

Mitchell strode into the ring, the unicorn cantering around it. There was one tiny, ugly moment when the unicorn reached its muzzle over to eat a little girl's ice cream cone, but Alicia was able to restrain the creature.

They left the arena as Lucy strode to the centre of the mudpit in a black leather jumpsuit. It looked like she'd raided Catwoman's outfit from the *Batman* movie.

"Ladies and gentlemen, welcome to this special night of World Wide Wrestling, brought to you by my generosity." She waited for applause, but the crowd became confused. She was looking and acting weird.

"I know you all want to see mud." She paused. "Do you want to see mud?"

The crowd went along with her now and screamed approval at everything she said. Mitchell stood, trying not to react as he heard his mother's voice coming out of Lucy's mouth.

"And do you want to see blood?" she asked.

That shocked the crowd. But it didn't stop them from suddenly chanting and cheering. "Blood! Blood! Blood!"

Across the ring, Mitchell caught Whip's eye. His lover was already muddied and he was scratching his arms. Mitchell sent a telepathic message that it was a side effect of the heat-treated mud.

Lucy said, "But tonight, in honour of this so...very special fight, we have two fighters! Mitchell 'Mudpit Madman' Dykins and Whip 'Mudshark' Jackson!"

Mitchell went to join Whip but Lucy held up her arm.

"But wait! There's more! We don't have two fighters. What am I saying? We have four!"

With a pop, Friday Otis Doombringer appeared in the ring beside Whip's alter ego. It was Mitchell's Uncle Foti, looking helpless and blind one second then looking the picture of health the next.

Both Whip's alter ego and Foti began attacking Whip. The crowd went berserk, loving it.

They kept chanting for blood as Mitchell tried to race across the ring, Lucy's hand jolting him with a high-voltage charge. She was carrying a Taser.

With the crowd's screams in his ears, Mitchell dropped face first into the mud. He tried to pull himself out, but the Mongolian death worm's face appeared as he raised his head, gasping for breath.

It was his mother.

He rolled out of the way but the worm was huge and heavy. And suddenly Justice Lashdown, a maniacal leer on his face and dressed in lederhosen, joined the worm in battle.

The worm kept wrapping itself around Mitchell's body, Lashdown jolting him with a cattle prod. Mitchell kicked the judge in the chin. The prod and the man holding it careened right out of the ring, head first into a cement post. Lashdown crumpled in a heap. Mitchell kept struggling with the worm.

He was sure he heard his ribs breaking. He fought the worm, waiting for the Marshals to come and rescue him.

"Hit her in the head!" he heard Whip's voice in his head.

Mitchell began to pound the worm that sang nursery rhymes in his head.

"Fuck you!" he screamed at her, getting on top of the worm, pounding its head in the mud. The Marshals stormed the ring. It took six men to pin down Foti and Whip's alter ego. They were carried away in golden shackles.

The beast bitch of a worm was a different story.

Whip was with him now, tackling the worm's body.

"He doesn't love you. He'll fuck anything that moves," the worm sneered.

Mitchell ignored her. He began shovelling hot mud into the worm's mouth. The Marshals jumped back into the ring, one of them dropping a giant golden anvil on the worm's head. Her shrieks and jeering stopped. Blood splattered from her caved-in head all over Mitch, Whip and the Marshals.

Then the insane itching began.

The crowd was having a blast, but still the bitch didn't die. It took three more body slams and a lot more gushes of blood but then she was gone. Slumped into a corner of the arena, Lucy lay in a daze.

"What's going on?" she asked, not realising she still held the microphone in her hands.

Whip dragged Mitchell to his feet and raised both their hands to the crowd.

"Blood! Blood! Blood!" the crowd chanted.

Mitchell bowed, longing to stick his hand down his pants and give his boy bits a really good scratch.

Whip led him out of the ring. "My balls are on fire," he muttered. "And not in a good way."

* * * *

Mitchell sat on the white-gold sand of Havens Beach, a tiny coastal town in Sag Harbor, New York, staring out to sea. It had been two months since the fight. Two months in which the WWW offices had been taken over by Whip and Mitchell to use as sports educational facilities for children and young adults with what were perceived as physical handicaps.

Foti, Justice Lashdown and Goyathlay Damek were still under strict medical supervision in a secured hospital in Teotihuacán. None would be approved for release any time in the immediate future, according to Justice Tillman.

The wicked witch Kathy was dead. The worm had been burned, the mudpit from the bout cleansed and buried deep in an unknown location.

Lucy had been treated as an outpatient, and thanks to Christopher and Daine's culinary intervention, was happily enjoying blueberry icing and a hot new relationship with Njáll in the deep heart of Connecticut's wetlands.

Apparently, she and Commander Jørgensen shared a love of, er…nature and, um…dung.

WWW would still stage benefit shows, all of the proceeds going to children's charities. Its new purpose to help people who had mobility issues had been Alicia's idea, one that had been blessed by Copper and Ember.

With Alicia in charge of classes for children, Whip and Mitchell had assigned Cinder and Aden Hephaestos to teach the young adults, and their sister Shula was in charge of adult education programmes.

Mitchell had watched with a heart bursting with joy as his sister had fallen for Cinder, who in turn had fallen in love with her. It was swift and it seemed very real, completely nurturing. Neither Mitchell nor Alicia wanted to return to the sad house in San Francisco. They would rent it out fully furnished and would pay somebody to pack their personal belongings and ship them to the east coast.

Neither of them ever wanted to set foot inside the house again.

He and Whip had found a gorgeous house for Alicia in Park Slope, right on the water, her bedroom window overlooking a gigantic cherry blossom tree. She had fallen for the tree first, then the house. As a child she'd never been able to climb trees. Now she sat in one for hours on end, watching boats in the harbour.

She and Shula were best friends already, and Cinder, of course, was there quite a lot.

Then they focused on each other. Mitchell and Whip had been at their new house for two hours, and so far all Mitchell had seen of it was the entryway where Whip had dive-bombed him, fucking him the second they walked through the door.

And now they were here on the beach of Whip's dreams. It had taken seven weeks of the two of them dreaming together to catch special glimpses of the place. They'd drawn images of the house that dwelt there in both their minds. Then, sheer luck—no, divine superpower intervention—had led them to taking a drive from New York City up the coast.

They'd stopped in tiny sea ports, even taken a prop plane to Fire Island. But in his heart Mitchell didn't think their beach was just a gay one. He wanted it to be a beach that Alicia and Cinder, should they wind up married and having a family, would feel comfortable bringing their children to.

A chance meandering online had led to a new listing in Havens Beach, Sag Harbor. It was a six-bedroom cliff-top property with unobstructed views of Shelter Island across the bay and the town of North Fork and the outlying areas of Connecticut.

It had huge windows and ceilings, rooms filled with art and fireplaces.

The property had a swimming pool and private trails into the parklands surrounding it. Mitchell could already picture bringing friends and students here for weekend retreats. They would spend their weekdays in Manhattan but this was their sanctuary. Their wonder world.

"That's it," Whip said the second he saw the video tour on the Realtor's website, his face awash with tears. "That's the beach. See how private it is? We can sunbathe nude. And look, there are stone steps from the house right down to the water, but you need a key for the gate. It's so private and so safe."

They'd viewed the video countless times. They'd showed it to Alicia and discussed it with her on Skype, but Whip's very emotional reaction to it had convinced her and Mitchell they should buy it sight unseen because three other people had already bid on it.

And now the simply breathtaking house was theirs.

They were here and Mitchell's soul felt peaceful.

"You think she'll marry him?" Whip asked.

"I hope so. I see how she looks at him. I like him for her."

"When I look at them, I see children with *her* lovely face and his bright red hair," Whip said. "Open your mouth, sweetie. I have a surprise."

Mitchell dutifully opened. He caught a glimpse of brown and gold as Whip's fingers dipped against his tongue. The taste was sublime. Chocolate heaven. But wait…was that gold leaf he was eating?

Whip had brought a huge pie down to the beach. They had two more frozen mudpies inside for the days ahead.

Mitchell felt his cock hardening.

"It's a sex pie!" Whip shouted. "And I want to fuck you like a mad bunny!"

He was on top of Mitchell in seconds.

"I love you," Mitchell said, enjoying the taste of pie on Whip's tongue.

"You should. I'm pretty groovy." Whip laughed. It was so good to see him relaxed and happy. Well…parts of him were relaxed.

"I feel water on my toes," Mitchell said, gazing up at his man. Whip's tears were back. It was the moment they both remembered from their dreams. The moment that held them together.

"I do believe this is where Burt Lancaster fucked the bejeezus out of Deborah Kerr in *From Here to Eternity*," Mitchell murmured.

"Darling…he kissed her… He didn't fuck her. And he was wearing waist-high panties. Let me show you how a man fucks the love of his life."

Whip rocked against him as their cocks rubbed together. Mitchell heard a cry and a flap of wings. The eagle from his dream.

"I want that ass," Whip snarled. He let his cock rub down Mitchell's crack.

Mitchell loved the feeling of it, his whole body responding to every thrust.

Whip leaned on one elbow, continuing to feed Mitchell with his fingers. Water lapped at Mitchell's ass. He face felt hot as if his internal temperature was on broil then…bliss.

Ecstasy overtook him as Whip rubbed something wet on his hole. Whip was whispering to him but Mitchell wanted to get fucked. He pushed his lover back and rolled onto his belly.

"I need it," he said over his shoulder, his cock grinding against the sand.

Whip put love bites across Mitchell's tailbone. Mitchell felt them ripple through his whole body—even his nipples were rock hard. Whip tore into him, gripping Mitchell's hips. The sensation of the cold water, the hot cock and whatever the hell had been in the pie made Mitchell come with a roar. He got to his knees, Whip kneeling between them, relentlessly fucking him, his cock moving into him like a hot knife through butter.

Mitchell sighed with contentment but Whip stopped moving. He told Mitchell to turn over. Both men hated it when Whip slipped out of him but he quickly rectified that as soon as Mitchell was on his back again.

Whip bent his head and kissed Mitchell as he began fucking him again.

He moved his head down, gently sucking Mitchell's nipples. Mitchell loved the way Whip came in a rush, his mouth on his, fingers squeezing the tip of Mitchell's left nipple. Mitchell reached between them and pulled on his cock. His ass clamped down on Whip's cock as he spewed fresh hot juice between their bodies, Whip fucking him with steady, deep thrusts.

For several minutes afterwards, they kissed each other, nibbling at the pie. Whip rolled off him. Their cocks were still hard.

"Is it me or magic?" Mitchell asked, reaching over to touch his lover's shaft.

"You, baby." He held his fingers to Mitchell's mouth. "And maybe a little...just a little...magical mudpie."

About the Authors

A.J. Llewellyn

A.J. Llewellyn lives in California, but dreams of living in Hawaii. Frequent trips to all the islands, bags of Kona coffee in the fridge and a healthy collection of Hawaiian records keep this writer refueled.

A.J. never lacks inspiration for male/male erotic romances and on the rare occasions this happens, pursues other passions such as collecting books on Hawaiiana, surfing and spending time with friends and animal companions.

A.J. Llewellyn believes that love is a song best sung out loud.

Serena Yates

I'm a night owl who starts writing when everyone else in my time zone is asleep. I've loved reading all my life and spent most of my childhood with my nose buried in a book. Although I always wanted to be a writer, financial independence came first. Twenty-some years and a successful business career later I took some online writing classes and never looked back.

Living and working in seven countries has taught me that there's more than one way to get things done. It has instilled tremendous respect for the many different cultures, beliefs, attitudes and preferences that exist on our planet.

I like exploring those differences in my stories, most of which happen to be romances. My characters have a tendency to want to do their own thing, so I often have to rein them back in. The one thing we all agree on is the desire for a happy ending.

A.J. Llewellyn and Serena Yates love to hear from readers. You can find their contact information, website details and author profile page at http://www.total-e-bound.com.

Total-E-Bound Publishing

www.total-e-bound.com

Take a look at our exciting range of literagasmic™
erotic romance titles and discover pure quality
at Total-E-Bound.